HOME

TRUTHS

by

C J Richardson

Copyright © 2018 C J Richardson

All rights reserved.

ISBN-13: **9781717874894**

CONTENTS

	Acknowledgments	i
1	Brief Encounters	1
2	The Lost Princess	18
3	Lads' night Out	28
4	The Night Watchman	33
5	Walls	47
6	Centre of Attention	50
7	New Beginnings	56
8	Hidden Treasure	59
9	The Key to Freedom	76
10	Nursing a Grudge	92
11	Taking Time Out	108
12	Sweet and Sour	121
13	Life Stylist	130
14	Holding on to Faith	138

To my husband, John for all his continued love, support and understanding.

1 BRIEF ENCOUNTERS

1969

Barbara walked in through the shabby front door at the same moment, Mr Brylcream, her stepfather, was crossing the hall. The usual fug of diesel fumes surrounded him, making her gag. He looked at her briefly with dark beady eyes before turning away.

'I hear you got yourself in a right bloody mess,' he mumbled over his shoulder.

Mum had obviously told him. Barbara shook her duffle coat off her shoulders and hung it on the coat rail, adding it to the jumble of grubby anoraks, scarves, his donkey jacket and oily overalls. Is that it? All he's got to say? She looked at herself, side-on, in the cracked, hall mirror.

She entered the kitchen, her shoes immediately making contact with a sticky patch on the grubby, cracked lino.

Sheila was standing by the gas cooker, her figure still trim, her make-up perfect, her glossy, chestnut hair pinned up in rollers and kept in place by a paisley headscarf. A pan of homemade chicken soup bubbled on the back ring. Yesterday's leftovers. The smell of tripe and onions, emanating from the pot her mum was stirring, made Barbara gag again.

Sheila looked up briefly and nodded before turning back to the job at hand. The hurt was still evident in her sad grey eyes, but at least she didn't look angry. Barbara hoped all the shouting had finished.

Without speaking, Barbara turned and headed for the living room.

He was sitting on the slack settee: ginger chest hair protruding through the diamond holes of his string vest; his upper arms thick with muscles; pools coupon and pen in his dirty hands, leaning forward, his paunch resting on his lap. David Coleman was reading out the football results on the telly. Barbara picked up the needles holding Mum's latest knitting project, a cable knit sweater for him. The straw-coloured wool was thick and course on her hand as she placed it on the arm of the only other comfy chair in the room. Lowering herself slowly, she tried not to make a sound, but the cushion wheezed as it deflated under her weight. Barbara heard a loud 'Tut'. Holding her breath, she waited a moment then picked up her mum's knitting pattern book and leafed through the pages.

*

The Old Bridge Cafe was full, the air warm and thick with cigarette smoke.

Barbara and Louise were standing at the jukebox, two-shilling piece at the ready. Barbara patted down the lank brown hair that was wet through and sticking to her scalp. The bottom half of her bell-bottoms were cold against the back of her legs, soaked from trailing through the wet streets; the hems frayed from continually catching them with the heels of her shoes.

'Crikey, Babs, he's old enough to be your dad,' said her best friend, taking a peek at the man with thick black hair, sideburns and handlebar moustache who was sitting at the table behind them.

Barbara elbowed her. 'Louise Kennedy! I said don't look now!'

'Never mind him! What do you want?'

Barbara ran her finger over the lists. She trembled, knowing he was still watching her. 'I'm having *Dizzy*. I love Tommy Roe.' They keyed in their selections and went over to the counter. Mr Patel was wiping his glistening forehead with a dirty, stained tea-towel. 'Two glasses very hot Vimto. Yes?'

'We'd better make it last,' Barbara said as they made their way over to a window seat and sat down. Cupping the hot drinks to warm their hands, she added. 'I'm skint now.'

'Don't worry. Pete'll be here soon.'

'I'm not sure,' Barbara said, wiping the steamy window and peering into the darkness. 'I might give the Fair a miss. It's still chucking it down and I'll be in for a right shouting match if I'm late home again. Besides, I'm fed up of playing gooseberry.'

She could still see the gorgeous, dark-haired man over Louise's shoulder. He had put his booted feet up on another chair and was leaning back, his hands behind his head. His cobalt-blue eyes flashed with mischief as he smiled at her again. He mouthed the words to the song "*I'm so dizzy, my head is spinning. Like a whirlpool, it never ends, and it's you girl making it spin*". Her insides somersaulted. She couldn't believe he was actually aiming his words at her.

Louise put her hand on Barbara's arm, frowning. 'Doesn't your mum stop him having a go?'

She forced herself to look directly at her friend. "She won't be there tonight. Mum's got a new job cleaning down at the Town Hall. She doesn't get home 'til about midnight.'

'C'mon. We could scrounge a lift back. My dad would come and get us if I asked him.'

Mr Gorgeous coughed and sat up, putting his feet back on the floor. 'Hey! Don't mean to butt in, but I could give you a lift. What time will your boyfriend get here?' he asked, turning to Louise.

'Err. Anytime now,' she said, gawping at him, twirling her long blonde hair around her finger and fluttering her eyelashes.

Barbara felt a familiar disappointment. Louise had done it again. It was always the same. Her face burned as she choked the words out, trying her best to sound nonchalant. 'It—it's alright,' she said. 'We can manage.'

'Hope I'm not interrupting anything?'

'Pete!' shouted Louise and jumped up to fling her arms around her boyfriend's neck and kissing him fully on the lips. No one had heard him come in.

Mr Gorgeous turned his smile back to Barbara, making her blush. 'Honestly. It's not a problem.'

'Aye. Aye. What's going on here then?' said Pete, pulling Louise's arms from around his neck. He looked from Steve to Barbara and back again.

Mr Gorgeous took hold of Barbara's hand and

squeezed it. 'I'm Steve,' he said to Pete. 'Your personal chauffeur for the evening.'

Barbara didn't know which way to look. The palm of her hand tingled as a jolt of electricity shot through her stomach. The thought of going in his car excited her. No one on her street owned a car.

*

Sheila poked her head around the living room door and smiled when she saw Barbara looking at her knitting pattern book. Looking over at the telly and seeing and hearing David Coleman, she went back into the kitchen.

Barbara followed her. 'It's finishing,' she said. 'Can I have my tea in here?'

'Don't be daft. You'll come and sit in there with Dad and me,' Sheila said, ladling soup into two bowls.

Barbara hated it when she called him Dad. Gerry, dirty, disgusting Gerry. Not Dad. 'I don't want to sit in there. I'd rather be on my own.'

Her mother ignored the comment and pulled out a loaf, cutting several slices off and putting them on a plate. 'I'll carry your dad's tea through. You bring the soup,' she said, holding the plate of tripe in one hand and bread in the other. Barbara picked up the piping hot bowls and followed on, fidgeting as the heat started to burn her fingers, waiting while her mother backed into the living room door to open it.

'About bloody time,' said Gerry. 'I was beginning to think my throat had been cut.'

'I didn't want to disturb you when you were checking your pools,' Sheila said, in that lovey-dovey voice Barbara hated. As she put the plate on his coffee table along with the bread, Gerry gave her bottom a squeeze. She giggled and slapped his hand. 'Cheeky,' she said.

Barbara hopped about from foot to foot, the heat from the bowls almost unbearable.

Taking two slices of bread for her and Barbara, Sheila made her way over to the dining table under the window on the far wall and pushed the usual clutter of knitting patterns, make-up and magazines to one side. The thin, floral-patterned curtains had been drawn to block out the dark, cold night. Barbara almost dropped the bowls onto the blue-checked, plastic tablecloth in relief.

'Ouch!' she yelped, blowing her fingertips and waving her hands frantically.

'Watch what you're doing,' he yelled. 'Bloody great lump.'

Barbara swallowed hard, his voice ringing in her ears, her eyes and fingertips smarting. Sitting down, she spooned some soup from the edge of the bowl, blowing it several times before gingerly putting it to her lips and sipping.

'No need for that, Gerry,' her mum said, patting Barbara's hand. 'Take no notice, love. It's because he hasn't won anything,' she added, turning to face him. 'I wish you'd throw your money at me like that.'

'I can throw you on the bed if you like.'

Sheila laughed. 'Mmm. That sounds more like it.'

Barbara wished her mum wouldn't behave like that. How could she even like him? Getting up from the table, Barbara felt the bile rising. 'Sorry. I...' She held her hands over her mouth, dashed from the room and up the stairs. She barely had time to put her head over the toilet bowl before the retching started.

'That's what you get for behaving like a tart,' she heard him shout from the bottom of the stairs a few minutes later. 'Should have learned to keep your knickers on.' The sound of a plate clattering in the kitchen sink was swiftly followed by the slamming of the front door. He'd gone. Barbara breathed a sigh of relief.

*

They were on the way home from the fair and she couldn't believe he was taking Louise and Pete home first, that she was sitting in the front of the tiny Fiat, that it was her friends squeezed in the back. Who was she kidding? She knew the real reason was her size.

As they travelled, Steve rested his hand on her knee between gear changes. It made her shiver. She relived the whole evening in her mind: him holding her hand on all the rides; buying her candyfloss; winning the teddy bear she was holding on to as if it were made from gold. She would treasure it forever. Wow! My first boyfriend and he's twenty-three. Barbara wanted to giggle out loud.

She was still in a daze when Steve jumped out of the car and pulled his seat forward so Louise and Pete could climb out.

'Byeee,' shouted Louise, waving and grinning like a loony. Barbara had a rush of self-doubt when they'd gone and started to panic. It was as if she had a frog in there, trying to escape, thudding against her ribs.

Steve climbed back in and the couple set off again. 'Where to?'

Barbara spun around to face him. 'I-I can't. I need to get home.'

'I meant home,' he said, putting his hand on her arm. 'Where is it?'

Barbara blushed, feeling foolish. 'Oh. Bradley Street. Near the Co-Op.'

'Hey,' he said, putting his hand back on her thigh. 'I'm not going to bite you. There's nothing to be scared of.'

The warm hand made her feel an ache deep down inside. 'I'm not scared. I'm worried about what my d...stepdad will say. What time is it?'

'It's only about eleven. Not too late.' He squeezed her knee.

Barbara felt sick. 'I'm supposed to be in by ten,' she mumbled, afraid he'd laugh at her.

Steve turned left at Bridge House and stopped on the narrow stone bridge to give way to an oncoming motorbike. The girl, riding pillion, had her head buried in the biker's back, her arms tight around his waist. It was Mary Gladstone. She lived two doors down from Barbara. It made her smile. She'd soon have her own stories to tell about where Steve had taken her. The thought made her giddy.

The cafe lights were still blazing on the south side of the river. Barbara looked over the wall at the water racing under the stone arches. The rain had stopped a couple of hours ago, but the water level was still rising.

Steve pulled up alongside the tree-lined, park entrance, a few streets from where she lived. The moon was behind a cloud and there were no street lights. She had been daydreaming and when he spoke, it made

Barbara jump.

'Is he okay with you?'

'Sorry?'

'The wicked stepfather. Is he okay with you? He doesn't knock you about, does he?

'Doesn't like me, or my sisters.'

'Older or younger?' Steve asked, his breath, warm and smelling of cigarettes blew softly on her cheek. He stroked her hair before pushing it behind her ears.

She shivered, not sure if it was fear or anticipation. 'Both older. Our Marge works in the typist pool down at the council offices. She's the one who got Mum the cleaning job. She shares a flat with a couple of girls, lucky thing. Jean's married. It's been worse since they left.' It felt good to talk to someone about it. Someone who was a grown up. 'He's only got me to pick on now.'

*

'I've made a cuppa,' Mum shouted up the stairs. 'It'll help settle your tummy.'

Barbara sat up on the iron-framed bed and lowered her feet onto the brightly-coloured rag rug, holding her prize teddy close to her chest, wondering why Steve hadn't been in the cafe since that night. Putting the bear on the pale-yellow, brush-nylon pillow, she dragged herself back downstairs. Her mum had stoked the fire and now it blazed brightly in the hearth. She sat down on the settee, glad he'd gone out.

Sheila looked up from her knitting and smiled. 'Don't take it to heart. He didn't mean what he said, you know. It's a bit of a shock for him. He'll come round. Give him time to get used to the idea.' Barbara didn't respond. 'We'll get through this, you'll see,' she said. 'It'll be wonderful to knit for a baby again.'

'What?' Barbara's eyes widened. She felt faint.

'I'll do yellow and white. No point in pink or blue, is there? Don't want to waste money.'

'I can't,' she mumbled, swallowing the bile in her throat.

'Can't what?' her mother asked, absently taking a sip of tea and staring into the fire. 'It'll be strange having a little one around.' Taking up her needles again, she continued to reminisce. 'Eeh. I remember your dad when you came along. The look on his face every time he picked you up. "We should call her Celia," he'd said. He were a right softie.'

Barbara saw the faraway look in her mother's eyes. She hadn't talked about her father since Gerry had moved in. 'Celia?'

'Yeah. Bit daft really. Reckoned he felt like Trevor

Howard whenever he looked into your eyes. Like the film: Brief Encounters.'

Brief Encounters? It had a familiar ring. Stirred a distant memory. 'Why didn't you?'

'What?' Her mum swapped the knitting over in her hands and started a new row, needles clicking loudly in the quiet room.

'Call me Celia?' The name sounded soft in her mouth. Barbara felt a rush of warmth as if someone were holding her close. She looked at the mantelpiece, trying to visualise Dad and Mum's wedding photo that once sat there. Their happy faces.

Sheila laughed. 'It reminded me of a woman up the road when I was a kid. She was stick-thin and had a vile temper. She used to have a different man every night. Everyone called her Celia Slut.'

Barbara flinched. Felt dirty.

*

'How can he not like someone as lovely as you,' Steve said, taking her hand and kissing it. He was looking straight into her eyes. She looked away. 'Hey. I won't hurt you. What's the matter?'

'Nothing. I was thinking how nice it was. Boys...Men don't normally—'

'Come here,' Steve said, pulling her to him, hugging her, kissing her forehead. Barbara nestled into his chest, the fine cord of his beige jean-jacket pushing into her face, the metal button on the pocket cold on her cheek. His hand stroked her leg while his mouth worked kisses down her face until, lifting her chin, he found her lips. He kissed her gently at first, and she responded eagerly until his tongue had worked its way into her mouth. Fumbling with the zip on her jeans, he slipped his hand inside her pants. Barbara pushed him away. 'I can't. I've never...'

He pulled her back to him, his voice throaty and breathless. 'It's alright. I'll look after you.' He tried to drag her jeans down. 'I'm glad I'm the first.'

'No! Please! No!' she begged.

Steve stopped, his face flushed. 'Jesus! Anyone'd think I was trying to kill you.' His eyes looked angry.

'I'm sorry. I didn't know you'd...' She pulled her jeans up and fastened them. 'Please take me home.'

'Sure,' he spat, pushing her back roughly. Starting the engine, he set off at speed. 'You need to be careful. You'll get yourself into trouble coming on to a man like that.' They pulled up at the corner of Barbara's street. 'You'd better get out here. I don't want your stepdad having a go at me as well.' He leant across her and pushed the passenger door open.

She looked at him, tears spilling over. She'd made a mess of everything! 'I'm sorry,' she whimpered. 'Will...Will I see you again?' His shoulders relaxed as he sighed. He forced a smile and took her hand. 'Course. I'd like that. Sorry for going off on one. It's not easy... you know...when it gets... I'll see you at the cafe next week.' He kissed her gently on the mouth. The ache started to tug away at her insides again as she responded to his touch.

*

'I'm not keeping it,' she blurted out. 'I can't.'

Her mum stopped knitting. She put it down and went over to sit next to her daughter on the settee. 'Now look,' she said, taking hold of Barbara's hands. 'Look at me.' Barbara raised her blurred, shiny eyes. 'I know it's a bit of a shock and yes...I thought that at first, but now I've got used to the idea...looking forward to it. And you will be too.' Barbara shook her head vehemently, her face screwed tight as her mother continued. 'Gerry'll make a wonderful grandad. He sounds angry, but he's such a softie under all that bluster. You haven't actually given him a chance. He reckons you're jealous of how much he loves me. You're not, are you? ' When her mum raised her finely plucked eyebrows, it made her look startled rather than puzzled.

'Jealous?' Barbara couldn't believe what she was hearing. 'I'm not jealous. I'm scared. He—'

'You need a bit of time to adjust, that's all. There's nothing to be scared of. I'll look after you. You'll have to tell me the father's name, though, Barbara...when you're ready. He has responsibilities too.'

'Please, Mum. Don't make me keep it.' She was sobbing now, snot running down her top lip. She could taste it as it seeped into her mouth.

'Now you listen to me, young lady. What's done is done. It's not the child's fault. You should have thought about what might happen before you got carried away with some lad.'

*

Barbara got out of the car. Steve left her standing on the pavement under a street light. She didn't see her stepdad go back into the house and close the door. She couldn't see much of anything; her head was spinning.

The door flew open as she put her key in the lock.

'Where the hell have you been? Get in!' he snapped, slamming the door shut behind her. She flinched, looked at the floor, pushed past him to get to the stairs. He grabbed her arm. 'Don't think I don't know what you've been up to. I saw you getting out of lover boy's car.'

Barbara struggled to get free, but he tightened his grip.

'Ow! You're hurting me. Get off!'

He swung her around, grabbing her chin with his free hand. She saw the spittle gathering at the corner of his mouth, her nostrils filled with the acrid smell of diesel, the stench of beer on his breath. 'I bet you didn't tell *him* to get off, you little tramp. Enjoy it? Think you're all grown up?' His lips curled into a sneer. 'Let's see how grown up you really are.'

2 THE LOST PRINCESS

2006

I climbed the rungs as Robert steadied the ladder. I hadn't set foot on a ladder in years, and I didn't feel particularly comfortable doing it now. Arthritis in my hip made me wince a little as I negotiated the narrow rungs. Gripping the torch, I stepped up into the vast space of the attic. Robert joined me, and we directed our lights; searching out all the nooks and crannies. Cobwebs hung from joists and rafters, and a fine grey film cloaked the boxes and furniture. I wiped my hand across the top of a small cabinet and watched the dust motes dance in the beam of my torch.

'This is going to take some time.' I whispered to Robert who stepped carefully around the random shapes covering the floor.

'I know. But why are you whispering?'

'I don't know,' I laughed. 'It feels the right thing to do. Don't you think so? I feel like I'm intruding.'

Robert shone his torch around some chairs. He pulled back the dust sheets. 'I could probably do something with these,' he said. 'They're late Victorian or early Edwardian I think. The springs and stuffing seem sound enough. I could re-upholster them and sell them in the shop. They'd fetch about five hundred with a bit of work. What do you think?'

'I think your head's always at work. I'm not interested in the value of her things. I need to spend some time looking through them all before I make a decision about anything.'

'Of course, you do. I'll set up some lights so you can see properly. Leave it to me.'

We made our way back downstairs to the large, plainly furnished rooms and I wondered where all the magnificent pieces of furniture Mum always talked about had gone. I assumed Aunt Clara must have sold them. Why? Was it to provide herself with some extra income? She never kept in touch with us after Dad and Gran had died. Mum always said she was a bit of a snob and didn't want anything to do with us. And who was I to argue?

What a shock when I got the letter from the solicitors' to say I was the sole heir to Gran's estate now that Aunt Clara had passed away intestate and I was the only living relative! Mum told me Gran had died of a broken heart in the spring of 1946, after months of mourning when my dad hadn't come home from the war. I was only three at the time. We had been living with Gran at Bridge house during the blitz.

*

I locked the front door and walked across the gravel drive to the car, looking back at the walls covered in an autumn blaze of Virginia Creeper. Robert drove us home; back down the motorway, back to our perfect little retirement bungalow in Marchford on the outskirts of Oxford. At least that was what it was supposed to be, but getting Robert to sell the antique business was a bit like asking a fish to live on dry land. The Hotel chain had offered us a reasonable price for the house. I hoped that might help him change his mind.

Arriving home three hours later, Robert and I were both exhausted. As soon as we were inside, he lit the fire and went over to the Edwardian drinks cabinet to pour two small glasses of port.

I leaned back in my armchair and sipped my drink slowly, feeling it warm the back of my throat and dull the pain in my hip. He leaned forward and stoked the fire, setting the logs ablaze again.

I couldn't help wondering if it would be simpler if we got someone in to sort everything out after all. It was going to take weeks to do it ourselves.

Robert walked over to the cabinet and poured himself another drink 'You?' he asked, holding his glass up. I shook my head. The thing I wanted most right now was a hot bath.

*

Sitting on one of the chairs Robert had been admiring yesterday, I was on my third box of treasure. The first two contained official-looking documents, household receipts and so on. I decided to leave them for now and take them home to read. The next one was much more promising. It was full of old photographs.

'Ah! I've found some photos, Robert. We can take them home with us.' Robert gave a grunt of acknowledgement as he eyed up a silver tea service he'd found inside a small packing case.

There were pictures of my dad as a young boy. He was standing knee high at the side of a tall man with a stern expression and a well-manicured moustache. I guessed it was his father. There were pictures of him as a baby on his mother's knee, her face also serious. I think that was the way of things then. The fact that everything was in a deep shade of sepia didn't enhance mood or feeling. I wondered if they showed any emotion towards their children. I thought the chair in the photo resembled the one I was sitting on now. There were more photos of Dad as a teenager and, finally in colour, as a young man in uniform. He was so handsome. I had a copy of the same picture at home. Even when she married Ted when I was six, Mum always kept it on my bedside table so I could never forget what a fine man he was. "I'm your number two dad, Margaret," Ted would say. He was a kind and gentle man and I always felt very much loved by him. My childhood was full of happy memories.

Something didn't feel right. 'Why are there no pictures of Clara? It doesn't make any sense. I can't even remember what she looked like Robert. Mum didn't have any photos of her. I haven't come across any at all. Have you?'

'Don't think so,' he said. 'I don't remember seeing any. Your Aunt Clara doesn't seem to have anything that resembles a family tie.'

'I remember Mum telling me she was far too busy in London to come home even when Gran died and she left Mum to organise the funeral. She had obviously started a new life for herself.'

'I suppose she must have come back at some point. I wonder why she didn't marry.'

'I know, I wondered about that too. Mum said she was stunning and apparently in much demand by eligible bachelors. She never understood why Clara wouldn't answer her letters either. She used to say what lovely person she was until she went off to London.'

HOME TRUTHS

I searched the room for something that could possibly have belonged to her. I felt as if she was hiding from me. I wanted to see the face of this woman who snubbed my mother after Gran and her brother had died. I searched among the boxes and came across a sizeable oval picture frame: a portrait of a young woman gazing into the distance, her hair tight across her head, a twist of locks fastened low into the nape of her neck. She wore a chocolate-brown dress with a tight-fitting, buttoned-up bodice and a heavy bustle at the back. The woman wore a cameo brooch at her throat. There was a deep sadness in her striking green eyes. The small gold plaque at the bottom of the frame read, Constance Ryder 1856. A fleeting memory of the portrait hanging over the marble fireplace in the drawing room flashed through my mind.

'Ooh! What's that?' Robert took the picture and eyed it greedily. 'Mid 19th century. Could be worth a few hundred.'

I left him to it. I didn't remember it being referred to as an ancestor. Gran had purchased the burnt-out shell of the house in the early 1900's. Maybe it had been included in the sale because it had survived the fire. Mum said it had been empty for years and years. There had been rumours about a doctor who had lived there previously with his daughter and her husband. Apparently, the daughter had been quite mad, setting fire to the house in the middle of the night and they had all perished.

I noticed a significant trunk at the other end of the room and went to investigate. The initials on the side were CWG: my father's name, Cedric William Gardiner. I was so excited; my hand trembled as I lifted the lid.

Slowly unravelling the sheets of tissue paper, I lifted out a white, ermine stole. What would my father be doing with...? No. It must be Clara's trunk. The stole sent a shiver running down my back. A sudden flash of ermine and the sound of laughter...I had seen it before. When?

I slid back another layer of tissue and there lay a dress. A ball gown. I gently lifted it up to the light. It was so beautiful. A strapless, floor-length, taffeta ball gown... I felt the room spin as the door to my memories opened wide. I could hear her laughing, see her face in the soft light of my bedroom, the light catching the swirl of her rich plum coloured dress, the ermine stole stark against such a vibrant hue.

'Are you a real princess?' I asked, peeping out from under the covers.

'Oh Yes; my darling Margaret; I am a princess tonight. I'm going to a ball and I'm meeting Prince Charming. Your Aunt Clara feels like the most beautiful princess in the whole world.'

She waltzed around my bedroom. Her gloved arms conducting an imaginary orchestra. I felt dizzy with the sparkle of her. She was gliding. The diamonds around her neck and in her hair, dazzled and glittered.

'Will I be a princess when I grow up?'

She bent over me and I could smell her sweet perfume as she kissed my cheek, her skin as soft as velvet.

'Of course, you will. You will be even more beautiful than I am. Now, if you go to sleep for your Mummy and Granny like a good girl, I'll bring you a present from London when I go next week.'

'I will Aunt Clara, I promise.'

I squeeze my eyes shut, but I can still see the diamonds like stars against my eyelids. I'm sure I will never be able to sleep again...

*

'Oh, Aunt Clara...I do remember you,' I whispered as I looked down and stroked the dress draped over my knee. I tried to relive the moment, recall more detail, but the memory had faded.

I dipped further into the trunk and pulled out a small box. It was full of photographs. All of Aunt Clara; a baby; a toddler; a young girl and then, the most beautiful young woman I had ever seen and at the bottom of the pile were two newspaper clippings. They were yellowed with aged.

London Times Nov 15th, 1945

DEBUTANTE BADLY INJURED IN CAR ACCIDENT.

Miss Clara Winifred Gardiner was seriously injured in a car crash at the weekend. Miss Gardiner had recently become engaged to Mr Frederick Plant of, 'Plant's Nautical Engineering Company'. She is making a slow but steady recovery at Guy's General Hospital and should be allowed home in a few days. It is said that there has been irreparable damage to her face. Mr Plant, who had been driving at the time, was unavailable for comment.

London Times Feb 14th, 1946

SHIPPING ALLIANCE

Mr Frederick Plant of 'Plant's Nautical Engineering Company' announced his engagement to Lady Isabelle Worthington daughter of Lord Charles Worthington the shipping magnate.

The wedding will take place on 20th March at 2.00pm All Saints church, Notting Hill.

3 LADS' NIGHT OUT

1990

Norman licked his fingers and teased the errant strands of silver hair across his bald pate.

'You'll do,' he said to his reflection in the bathroom mirror. He leaned forward to check for any bits of food that might be clinging to his top denture.

Whistling softly, he made his way downstairs and into the sitting room where Dot was knitting a new cardigan in blossom-pink wool. Her eyes were glued to the telly.

'Alright, goggle-eyes?' he asked, as he made his way through to the kitchen. The thick and earthy, Tuesday-night smell of liver with an onion gravy made Norman's mouth water.

'You should watch it,' replied Dot, swapping her needles and starting a new row. 'That Billy Appleton's having an affair with Jack Charlesworth's wife. The mucky pair. It's disgusting.'

'It's only a programme, Dot. They're not really having an affair.'

Dot called through to him. 'Tea's in the oven. You'd better have it before you go. It won't keep.'

'Sorry, love, I don't want to be late. I'll turn the oven off and eat it cold when I get in.' He looked down at his black-leather slip-ons, all polished and waiting on a sheet of the Evening News by the back door. He still took great pleasure in being able to see his face in them. It always shocked him to see the state of kids' footwear these days. No pride in their appearance. A spell in the army would soon sort that out. It hadn't done him any harm. In fact, his best memories were from his time in the army. He knew most people looked back at the Falklands with scant feelings; it hardly got a mention when it came to the annual memorials. Maybe it wasn't a world war, but it had certainly felt like it to Norman out there on the front line. Out in all weathers. Pushed to the limit. Looking after all those young men. "Stand by your beds, Lads. Atteeen-tion!" "Yes, Sarge. No Sarge. Kiss my backside, Sarge." They thought he didn't hear, giggling like schoolboys. Then he'd send for them and watch them shake. Lads today couldn't stand a bit of discipline. Get the newspapers involved. Not like in his day.

He put his slippers down and pushed his feet into the shoes.

'Who are you playing against tonight?'

'The Dog and Duck.'

'Isn't that the other side of town?'

'Yeah. It'll be a late finish.' Norman took the keys out of his pocket and jangled them in the air. 'I've got my key so don't wait up,' he said.

'Aren't you forgetting something?'

'Sorry,' he said, going back into the sitting room. Walking over to his wife, he leaned over the back of the armchair and kissed the top of her head. Her soft perm tickled his face. He breathed in her delicate perfume. 'I don't know what I'd do without you. Night love.'

'Away with you. You're such a big softie,' she replied. Her eyes were still on the telly, but they lit up with pleasure.

He loved his wife dearly, all soft and warm like his mother. That's why he'd asked her to marry him. A home from home. He wished it could have been enough.

He stepped out of the back door and locked it,

leaving Dot safe and warm. The air was tight with frost as he pulled the brown, knitted scarf close around his neck. Striding out along the glistening pavements, he felt the moon watching him as he made his way across the river bridge and to the south side of the town. He preferred to walk. It gave him time to think. To anticipate the evening ahead.

*

When he reached the Dog and Duck, he stood outside for a few minutes, watching the darts game. The laughter and high spirits seeped out of the well-lit windows and the open door.

Norman slid back into the dark shadows and out of sight as a young woman stepped outside in a thin blouse and short skirt. She lit the two cigarettes protruding from her cherry-coloured lips, visibly shaking as she cupped her hands around the flame of her lighter. Norman could see a black, tattooed snake coiling around her left thigh. She was soon joined by a thickset man in a short-sleeved shirt. His biceps, melon-sized beneath his sunbed-tanned, orange skin, made Norman shiver.

The man batted his arms and stamped his feet. 'It's freezin' my knackers off.'

The woman's teeth were chattering as she spoke. 'I'll warm you up when we get back to mine.'

'I'll bet,' he said, pushing her up against the wall and shoving his free hand up her skirt.

The man fumbled with his zip unsuccessfully. He was unsteady on his feet and staggered back. 'Sod this for a game of dominoes. I'm going back inside.'

The woman straightened her skirt and followed him.

Norman was alone again. He blew his hands and rubbed them together to bring some feeling back to them. Turning his attention back to the window, he watched the darts game. Joe Barraclough had scored three triple tops, followed by a loud cheer as the ref shouted 'One hundred and eighty'. He made a note of who had turned up and checked the scores on the chalkboard to see who was winning. Satisfied his team were definitely the better players, Norman looked away and walked back in the direction he had come from. A few minutes later and he was turning left into Corporation Avenue.

*

A couple, arms linked, were coming towards him. He crossed the street and walked purposefully, head down, in the opposite direction. When they had gone, he waited for a few minutes more, looking up and down the street before slipping up a ginnel that led to the back gardens. There was a light on in the upstairs window of number seven. Picking up a bit of gravel from the lane running the length of the terraced row, he aimed and threw. The tinkling sound was answered by the bedroom light being switched off. In complete darkness, apart from the tip of the moon which was trying to peak over the rooftops at him, Norman made his way down the garden path and waited outside the back door. It opened only slightly, the warm air escaping and carrying a musky scent that drifted across Norman's face. He breathed it in and felt the swelling in his trousers harden.

'Come in, Sarge,' whispered a trembling voice.

'Don't mind if I do, Private Shackleton,' he said, grinning widely. The familiar, broad chest, bulging through the bright white vest, still made his heart race.

4 THE NIGHT WATCMAN

2017

The Night Watchman seemed to get taller and taller, his red eyes gleaming from under his black hood. He held his voluminous cloak wide, revealing a dark, navy-blue sky, dotted with a thousand stars. Jake could hear the blood pounding in his ears. He looked over to the hospital bed where his father lay unconscious, wired up to machines that beeped with each beat of his heart. Jake turned away, his chest tight with fear as he forced his feet to walk into the unknown. He didn't know if he would ever return. He didn't know if he would succeed in the Night Watchman's task. His dad's life depended on his success, as did his own. Taking a deep breath, he stepped into the void, the cloak wrapping around his back and closing behind him.

Beneath Jake's feet, the ground was soft and

squishy. As his eyes grew accustomed to the dark, he could see a vast landscape of low, rolling hills and deep crevices threading their way across the land like rivers, twisting and turning, making hills appear to be small islands.

The Night Watchman's words echoed in his head, jibing, threatening. "Remember...you have until the last star is extinguished and if you fail, you will both be mine forever."

Jake looked up and could see a few stars disappearing in quick succession. He shouted into the night sky. 'How long before they all go out?' No response. 'Which way should I go?' Total silence. He didn't know what to look for. Everything looked identical. Every small island hiding its own secrets. He stared hard at his surroundings looking for a clue, a sign, anything that might show the way. *Where would Dad's memories be kept? How would he know which was* the *right one?*

In the distance, what looked like a burst of electricity zigzagged from one small island to another, lighting up the dark for a second. As more flashes appeared, he noticed a small area where none occurred: a black patch where the stars had already gone out. *That was it. That's where Dad's memories had been lost. It must be. That's why it was so dark.* The Night Watchman had been clear, cruel, "Unless your father remembers the most important memory in his life, he will never wake from the coma."

Jake had agreed to the Night Watchman's challenge, and now he could only try his hardest to find the memories his dad had lost before it was too late. The tears were welling up again, but he snatched them away with the back of his hand. There was no time to feel sorry for himself. His dad's life depended on him.

He walked towards the patch of dark sky. It wasn't easy as the ground wobbled and rolled beneath his feet. The sensation reminded him of a family holiday in Scotland three years previously. He had been eleven at the time and they had visited a theme park. He'd played on giant inflatable pillows, bouncing up and down without shoes to avoid damaging them, his socks sliding on the smooth surface.

Sitting down, Jake took off his trainers and tied the laces together before hanging them around his neck. He began to run, bouncing across the fissures but his legs soon began to tire. He stopped and sat down again, catching his breath, rubbing his shoulder and wrist in turn as they throbbed. He was thinking about the accident, how it had all been his fault. The stars continued to flutter and die. Time was running out and he was already tired.

*

Jake jumped into the car, threw his rucksack on to the back seat and fastened his seat belt. The CD player was blasting out a Rod Stewart number when he waved goodbye to his mum.

'Hi, bud. Ready for a super cool weekend in the Lake District?' Tousling Jake's thick mop of black hair, his dad started the car and set off at speed, only having to slow down at the end of the high street. The new traffic light system had been put up outside the Coffee Stop Cafe just before the old bridge. 'That must be the twentieth time it's changed its name?' He said. 'I used to go in there all the time when I was in my teens.' Jake didn't bother answering as he watched the removal van rumble over the river at about five miles an hour.

Jake wished he would stop using words like *bud* and *cool*. It was embarrassing. 'Yes, Dad,' he replied, smoothing down his hair.

His dad turned down the music as they hit the motorway, immediately racing down the fast lane. Jake thought he heard a beeping sound. *How long before the questions start?* Jake started to count in his head. *One two three...*

Dad cleared his throat. 'How's Mum?'

Jake sighed. He'd get the same questions from Mum as soon as he got home. 'Fine,' he said, lifting his earphones and plugging them into the i-phone. Dad had bought it last week. Another 'guilt' present.

'Don't do that. I want to talk to you. Has your Mum

asked about me?'

Jake sighed again and put the headphones on his lap. 'Just the usual.' *What was that beeping?*

'Do you think she misses me?'

'Oh, Dad! How many times?' Jake picked the headphones up again. *Why don't they sit down and talk it through?* He put the headphones on and turned up the volume. His dad grabbed his arm, but Jake pushed him off, frowning at his father. 'Leave me alone.'

'Off,' yelled his dad, poking the headphones with his finger.

'Ouch! That hurt.' Jake pulled a face but ignored the command.

His dad turned towards him and pulled at the headphones. 'Take those bloody things off!' he shouted. The car veered across the motorway, the brakes screeched. Jake screamed as the vehicle careered towards the central barrier... BANG! Everything went black.

*

Jake couldn't breathe. Something was covering his face. He pushed and pulled, trying to move the heavy weight crushing down on him. A voice came out of the darkness. 'Take it easy, son. Try to stay calm. We'll have your dad off you in a minute.' The seat belt warning was still beeping.

*

Jake was sitting in the semi-darkness of the hospital room, his left arm in a sling. The doctor told him how lucky he had been not to be injured apart from a sprained wrist and whiplash. His father was lying on a bed.

'Your dad has a serious head injury, Jake,' the doctor said. 'We've telephoned your Mum. You can sit with him...wait together.'

Jake held his father's hand, trying not to look at the bloody bandage on his dad's head. Blood had always made him feel sick, faint even. Guilt was eating him up. If he had only listened to his father, none of this would have happened. 'I'm so sorry, Dad,' he whispered between sobs.

He heard the door opening and expected it to be his mum... but it wasn't. It was a tall figure wearing a dark cloak. He glided across the room, straight over to Jake who jumped out of his seat and backed into the corner. The figure came closer, looming over Jake's small frame. His foul breath filled Jake's nostrils, making him retch. 'Your father's time is up,' he said. 'I've come to claim him.'

Jake crouched down, trembling. His mouth was dry, his voice barely a whisper. 'Who are you?'

The man's eyes glowed red beneath his hood. 'I'm the Night Watchman. I take lost souls and keep them as my slaves.'

Jake screamed, pleading with him. 'No! Please! No! I'll do anything. Please!'

The Night Watchman's blood-red eyes gleamed. 'Are you *sure* you're willing to do anything?'

*

Jake opened his eyes. They were wet with tears. He had fallen asleep without knowing. He looked up at the sky again. Half of the stars had disappeared. *How could he have been so stupid?* The dark patch of sky was much more prominent now. Jake got to his feet and rubbed his painful shoulder. This place was making him so tired. He knew he couldn't risk falling asleep again, so he set off a bit more slowly, pacing himself. The nearer he got to the dark area, the less he could see and the faster the stars were going out.

He missed his footing, misjudging the width, as he bound over a wide crack and fell to the bottom with a thud. He had landed hard on his back, winding himself. It took him a moment or two to catch his breath as he looked up at the narrow strip of sky, now almost devoid of stars. The sides of the crevasse were steep but spongy like the surface. He couldn't get a decent hand or foothold to climb up the sides. He fell back against the opposite wall each time he tried.

Jake sank down to his haunches. He struggled to think. The panic rose up, belting the sides of his chest. He remembered the rock-climbing trip last year. It had been the last 'together' holiday. Tears pricked again. He and Dad had loved rock climbing. Mum always watched from the bottom, panicking until they had made it safely to the top. Part way up the rock face had been a narrow channel they had needed to climb. It had been smooth down either side with nowhere to put hands or feet. Dad had called it 'The Chimney' as he had squeezed into the space and shown him how to tackle it.

This crevasse was different, not stone, not hard. *He would do this. He could do this.* Jake stood up and stretched his arms out wide, pushing into the flexible walls. He winced at the pain in his shoulder and wrist. Steeling himself, he spread his legs wide and, one at a time, he placed his feet on the soft sides and inched his way up. Progress was painfully slow and each step took a long time. He tried to concentrate on other memories from the past. *Which of them was the most important? Which particular memory would make Dad realise what he had to live for? Of course! Mum. Mum was what he had to live for. He needed to find the memory of their wedding day. Then Dad would wake up.* He was angry with himself for not thinking of it sooner.

The sky was utterly black above him when he finally pulled himself over the edge and lay flat. His arms and legs ached so much, he was sure he wouldn't be able to walk another step. The pain in his shoulder now burned deep and travelled all the way down to his wrist. Looking up, he could see the remaining stars were far away from him now. This must be the place. The place he'd find the lost memories.

Feeling about in the darkness, Jake crawled around on his hands and knees, He wasn't sure what he was looking for, but sensed he would know when he found it. There didn't seem to be anything at all. Nothing but the same smooth, cushiony surface everywhere as he crawled along, sliding his hands along the ground. The air was thick and he could feel himself getting sleepier and sleepier. It would have been easy to lose concentration and close his eyes, fall into the black nothingness, forget about the distant stars flickering as they died. He wasn't crawling anymore. He was sitting on his heels and letting his hands sweep the ground on either side of him, like two metal detectors drawing semi-circles on barren soil. His head began to nod and he slumped forward in a heap. 'Yuk!' He came to with a start. His face had landed in something slimy. The air was thicker. Warm and sickly. The gloopy liquid slid down his face like treacle, coating his lips. His tongue automatically licked it away. He recognised the sour, metallic taste immediately and retched as his stomach somersaulted. He jumped to his feet. *Blood. Oh no! He couldn't. He couldn't.* He took a deep breath, trying to stop himself fainting. *You have to, he told himself.* He tried to kneel but stood up again quickly. *This is what's blocking Dad's memories. All this blood. C'mon Jake you can do it.* He forced himself to kneel down and searched again, gagging each time he put his hands through the pulsing, viscous slime. A sharp edge caught his fingers as he lifted something bulky and square.

He peered at the shape clutched between his hands. A small box with a lid. He wiped away the congealing substance and tore the top off. A great burst of light dazzled his eyes. The picture became clear. Mum and Dad were having a picnic by a river. It was a bright sunny day and they were laughing. Dad kissed Mum, but quickly, too quickly, the light faded. Darkness descended once more. Jake had no time for fear. He waded on his knees and found another box. Again, he tore off the lid. Another blinding light and Dad was dancing with Mum. They were at a party. The light went out. Another box and Dad was tearing along on a motorbike. Mum was riding pillion. Jake was so excited, he was getting nearer. Another box and Dad was at a different party with some teenagers. They were drinking Cola out of cans, joking and laughing, whistling and nudging each other as some girls arrived. The light went out. Jake looked up. There were only a few stars left. *Dad had looked so young. OMG! He was going the wrong way.* He needed to go forward in time to find the wedding day. *How much time had he got left? Which way?* Tears were stinging his eyes again. He shouted into the nothingness. 'Which way? Tell me...Please.'

The Night Watchman's voice thundered back. 'Your

time is running out. You'll soon be mine.'

'No! I need more time...please...please,' he pleaded, but there was no reply. Jake felt his way back, crawling on all fours through the repulsive mire, counting the open boxes until he reached the first one. He continued forward, his limbs aching with tiredness, his whole arm burning with pain. He found another box. The light blinded him for a second before he saw his mum and dad in a restaurant. He recognised it. "This is where I proposed to your mum," his Dad would say every time they went there for birthdays and anniversaries. He was sure he could smell the tangy hot cheese of his favourite Calzone pizza. His mouth watered. It was always Spaghetti Carbonara for Dad and Farfalle Salmone for Mum. Dad was giving her a small box. She spotted the ring and jumped up to hug him. Darkness fell again. *He must be nearly there now.* He crawled along determinedly, searching desperately and eventually found another box. His heart raced. *This must be it. It must be.* 'Please let it be the wedding day,' he said aloud, as he tore it open.

Light exploded in his face, flashes of electricity burst across the landscape, organ music pounded out a wedding march. He could see his mum walking down the aisle. He could see his dad waiting by the altar, smiling happily. He watched Grandpa give Mum away and sit down next to Gran who was dabbing her eyes with a hanky.

Jake jumped up. 'I found it,' he shouted. The Night Watchman cackled loudly. Jake swivelled around to find him standing behind him. He looked up into those red eyes. *Why was he laughing? He had seen the right memory, hadn't he? His Dad had to wake up.* The light began to fade. Jake dropped to his knees, sobbing.

'I hope you enjoy life in here, ' the Night Watchman said, laughing louder and louder.

Jake curled up into a ball, his hands covering his ears. 'I'm sorry, Dad. I'm so sorry,' he wailed. Too tired to try anymore, he sank into thick, tacky blood, drifting away into a deep sleep.

'Jake...Jake.'

It *sounded like Dad. It couldn't be.* He opened one eye and saw a faint beam of light a little way off.

The Night Watchman was standing over him, his red eyes boring down. 'Sleep, Jake. You're mine now. Sleep.'

It was so difficult for him to stay awake but...*that light. He needed to get to that light.* Jake dragged himself along.

'Forget everything, Jake. Go to sleep. Only ten stars left now. Nine...eight...'

Jake focussed on the shaft of light. He was getting nearer. 'Seven...six...five...' The Night Watchman's voice continued to count down the stars. Jake grasped the box. It felt warm against his palms and vibrated as if something was desperate to escape from it. It was so stiff. He couldn't do it. 'Four...three...two...one.'

The lid flew open and a baby cried, loud and clear, its voice echoing across the whole of the land. Light flooded the landscape. A blaze of electricity zigged and zagged, zipping over crevasses, dancing through the sky: a firework extravaganza. 'Jake. My beautiful, beautiful son.' Jake saw his dad lift a baby up and hold him close. Mum was sitting up in a hospital bed, her face flushed, her hair damp and clinging to her smiling face. The light didn't fade. Jake dragged himself to his feet. Had he finally found the memory that would wake his dad?

'Jake...Jake. Where are you? Are you okay?' Dad's voice sounded close now. So close.

Jake stared down at his hands and clothes as the blood ran off, leaving them spotless. The lake of blood all around him shrank and slid down into the fractures leaving the ground smooth and clean.

'Nooo!' screamed the Night Watchman. The red eyes disappeared leaving only a dark space under the hood. Jake grabbed the cloak, pulled it open and jumped back into the hospital room. His father still lay on the bed, eyes closed, calling for his son. 'Jake...Jake. Are you there?'

Jake ran to him. 'It's alright Dad. I'm here. I'm

here.' Dad opened his eyes and smiled at him. Jake rang the buzzer for help at the very same moment his Mum walked through the door. She pulled Jake close. 'Mum,' he cried, clinging to her.

Jake's mum took hold of Dad's hand and kissed it. He smiled at her. *It was going to be alright. Everything was going to be okay.*

5 WALLS

2015

They had moved into the small end terrace a few weeks ago. It had gardens to three sides, fenced off by a high wall. Beyond the wall, there was a school. It was the new Blackdale Academy, which Sarah attended. There was a primary school attached.

There was silence around the breakfast table as Sarah, her mother and her father watched the local news on television. A woman stood outside the school. She was crying, blinded by the flashes as the reporters took photographs. Her eight-year-old daughter had gone missing. Imogen had been wearing a pink dress and carrying her favourite book, *The Secret Garden,* when she disappeared on her way home from school.

Melanie Frost, Imogen's teacher, was visibly upset as she spoke in answer to the reporter's question.

'No. I haven't seen anyone suspicious hanging around outside the school. We make a point of watching as the children leave the school gates.'

Mrs Frost's husband had his arm tight around her shoulder, but she kept trying to shrug him off. Sarah saw a familiar fear in Mrs Frost's eyes. She glanced over at her mother. The reporter was saying that someone had seen Imogen cross over the bridge to the south side of town. She had been caught on CCTV passing the jewellery shop on the high street, but there had been no other sightings.

Sarah asked to be excused and went upstairs. She snatched up the book from her desk and threw it at the wall, the bile acid in her throat.

Some weeks ago, she had experienced terrible cramps and thought she was dying. She had been so relieved when her father had said it was because she was becoming a woman and he would no longer come and tell her bedtime stories. That's when the decision to move house had been agreed. It had been a shock when he had slipped into her room last night. She had pretended to be asleep when he put something on her desk. 'Something to read,' he had whispered before leaving.

Creeping into her parent's bedroom, she picked up the phone. Trembling, she knew what she had to do. Her father's words echoed in her head. *'If you even think about it, I'll know.'* She pressed out the numbers, her hands shaking.

When she had finished, she went back to her room and retrieved the book. Sitting on the top stair, she leant her back against the floral wallpaper and closed her eyes.

The doorbell rang.

On Friday, it was all over the national newspapers.

6 CENTRE OF ATTENTION

1969

We were in the Tower Ballroom that day. Mary had dragged me in; she watches that dancing-programme thing all the time. I don't know why. She's not exactly Verity Champagne. I said, 'Why do you want to watch that soppy stuff?' She said, 'Cos it's good, and besides, it's chucking it down and I got my hair done specially for this weekend.' I looked, but I couldn't tell. Didn't say so, though. Anyroad, it's not much fun in Blackpool when it's raining, so I said, 'Alreet. But I'd rather go to the pub and get a decent pint.' She said, 'I'm not sitting in a pub with all those hen-party girls giving you the glad eye.' I said, 'Don't be daft. Who'd look at me?' She said, 'Lots of women. You're a very attractive man, Leonard. I'm a very lucky girl.' I couldn't argue with that, could I? So we went to the Tower.

HOME TRUTHS

I spotted this girl as soon as we found a table and sat down. A flash of gold heels and a diamante dress, sailing around the dance floor with that poncey bloke. You know the one, Simon Whatdoyoumacallit. He dragged her out of the audience. I could see she weren't really sure, but he were. Too bloody sure - of himself - of his power over women. Wiggling his arse like he were God's Gift. All the women squealing like baby pigs trying to find a teat full of milk. He didn't want her. She were an excuse for him to show off. He picked up a microphone. He said, 'What's your name, Beautiful?' She went bright red, didn't know which way to look. He said, 'What's that? Speak up!'

He needed seeing to, embarrassing her like that. She said, 'Sophie.' It were like soft velvet the way she said it. I said to Mary; I said, 'Look what he's doing. Showing her up like that. Pulling her round.' Mary said, 'She wanted it. She wouldn't be dressed like that if she didn't, would she?' I said, 'Bollocks. She's just nicely dressed.' I looked at Mary in her jumper and jeans. I said, 'Likes to take care of her appearance.' She said, 'And I don't, I suppose?' Typical, Mary. Allus trying to start a row. I said, 'Are you trying to start a row or summat?' She said, 'I'm only asking if you think I don't take care of my appearance. That's all.' I didn't bother answering. If that Sophie were mine, I wouldn't treat her like that. I must have said it out loud or summat 'cos the next thing I know is Mary's jumped up from her seat and said, 'You fancy her, don't you?' I said, 'Don't be daft. I'm only commenting.' She said, 'Well, you can keep your comments to yourself or I'm going home.' 'Suit yourself,' I said, and she did. Left me sat there on my own, everyone gawping as she waddled her way through the rows of tables. I don't know how she thought she'd get home. No sign of any money when I forked out for petrol for the bike on the way here. I looked at the dance floor and copped a better look at Sophie as she made her way back to her table in Row A. It looked like she were out with her mam who stood up and kissed her, grinning like they'd won the lottery or summat. Just before she sat down, Sophie looked across the room and caught me gawping at her. I gave her that look that said, 'I understand your embarrassment. I'd never have put you through that if you'd been with me.' You know what I mean, the sort of look that speaks volumes. You'll have heard of people who can do that. That Mona Lisa were doing it in that picture what thingymajig painted. What's he called? Anyroad, I noticed that there were two free seats on the table next to her so I thought I'd saunter over there and slip into the one farthest from her. Didn't want to appear too keen.

She didn't look my way at first. Too busy watching all the other volunteers dancing. You could tell they were all 'up for it'. Not like Sophie. They jumped up as soon as Simon came anywhere near. I couldn't help looking at her. Her profile was as good as her full frontal. I mean face...you know what I mean. Anyroad, I

HOME TRUTHS

thought it were probably time to move up, so I shuffled my bum over and eased myself down onto the seat next to her. She turned to me. I could see the look of surprise. I said, 'You don't mind if I sit here do you?' She said, 'No.' Then she smiled. I knew I were onto a winner, so I said, 'Do you come here often?' Dead cool like. She said, 'Quite often. I love to dance.' I said, 'So do I.' As if. She didn't need to know I only came 'cos Mary pushed me into it. I mean, only ponces dance like that. I said, 'You must have been embarrassed when he dragged you out of your seat.' She said, 'I was. Can you imagine? Actually dancing with Simon Marvel.' I said, 'I suppose he's okay. I've seen better.' She said, 'Really? Who was that?' I said, 'Oh. Nobody you'd know. It were when I went to Benidorm last year. A Spanish feller.' She said, 'Wow! Was it Ricardo Montez?' I'd never heard of him, but I nodded. She said, 'Gosh. You're so lucky. How did you manage to get tickets? They're like gold dust.' She went all gooey-eyed then. She said, 'Perhaps you could take me to see him.' I said, 'Sure. I've got contacts. Danced with his partner. She were dead good.' Had to make her think I were worth summat, didn't I? She probably wouldn't look twice if she knew I danced more like Norman Wisdom than Fred Astaire. She said, 'You must be an excellent dancer if Maria Cortez was prepared to dance with you.' I said, 'I can do a bit when push comes to shove. Trained at Miss Clutterbuck's in Blackdale.' I remembered Kenneth Swainby, going there when we were in primary school. Right soft lad he were. We'd all called him Margo Ponstein after that ballet dancer. He'd allus cry and run home to his mam, the mardarse. Anyroad, it couldn't have been going any better until she said, 'We could have a dance when they ask the audience to get up. There's a knockout contest at the end.' I said, 'I'm sure we could find something better to do.' Her mam threw me a right dirty look. I said, 'Like a walk on the prom. It'll have stopped pelting down by now.' I said, it really loud so the old bag couldn't miss it. Sophie said, 'Don't be so modest. We'll easily win. I'm so glad you came and sat next to me. I've never danced with a professional before...well except for Simon.' I said, 'I'd love to, but I went over on my ankle a few days ago. It was when I were doing a jive. I were trying to lift a great big lass over my shoulder. Wonder I didn't break my back. I didn't want to hurt her feelings saying no to her. The doctor says I have to rest it.' Sophie seemed dead impressed. She said, 'That was very kind of you. We can do something slow. I promise not to stand on your toes.' To be honest, she were beginning to get on my nerves a bit by then, keep going on about it. I didn't feel like dancing. And anyroad, I were dog-tired after a week on night shift at the factory. I said, 'I just need to go to the you-know-what. I'll be back in a tick.' I squeezed myself through the tables. By heck, they don't half pack 'em in. No wonder Mary struggled. With her figure, it's not easy getting through tight spaces. I wanted to run when I got to the back, but I remembered about my ankle and began to limp until I got through the double doors and out into the foyer.

When I got outside, you'll never guess. Mary were still there, sitting on the steps. I said, 'I thought you'd have buggered off by now.' She said, 'Can't get into the room without a key, can I? Besides, I didn't want to leave you on your own.' I took her hand and pulled her up. She'd been crying. I can always tell when she's been crying. I pulled my hanky out and give it to her. I said, 'Wipe off them black streaks running down your cheeks.' She said, 'Thanks.' I told her to blow her nose as well; I can't stand a drippy nose. When she did and offered it back, I said, 'You can keep it. I've got a spare one back at the digs.' She said, 'You're so good to me' and pushed it into her anorak pocket. I felt a bit guilty, so I said, ' Do you fancy fish and chips, I'm starving?' She said, 'That would be lovely, thank you.' I knew I were still on a promise when she said that. She put her brolly up and held it over my head while she linked me. She's alreet is Mary. You know where you are with a girl like Mary.

7 NEW BEGINNINGS

1970

Barbara looks down at the cot beside her bed. The baby's asleep. Getting out from under the starched white sheets, she walks past the rows of beds and cots, deaf to the silly baby talk. The window is tall and wide and looks out onto a chalk-blue, June sky. She presses her finger to the windowpane and traces the white wisps of aeroplane trails to where they thin and disappear. She looks down the hill towards the town. People are sitting outside the Old Bridge cafe. She's pretty sure she can see Louise and Pete among them. Steve won't be there. Louise said he'd left town moved to somewhere on the south coast. His Uncle had a fruit farm and he was going to work for him.

'Miss Carter!' the nurse bellows down the ward. 'Your baby is ready for a feed. Come back to your bed immediately.'

Barbara turns to see all the Marrieds staring at her. As she makes her way back up the room, they all lower their gaze. She refuses to cry.

Climbing back into bed, she undoes her nightdress, releases the nursing bra and readies herself for the onslaught. The baby squawks, ugly and red-faced as the nurse keeps pushing it against Barbara's breast, tugging and pulling on the tender flesh until the baby latches onto the nipple. Barbara focuses her eyes on the blue expanse beyond the window at the end of the ward.

'You're not even trying, are you?' the nurse snaps. Barbara looks down at the blue-veined hand gripping her breast. She puts her arm under the baby's back.

'No! No! It's no wonder the child won't feed; you're barely holding him. Pull him close, make him feel safe.'

The murmuring starts up again, filling her ears. Barbara does as she is told, like a robot following instructions. The baby latches on, nipping and sucking. It's disgusting. A tiny *him*. How could they make her do this?

The nurse walks away and leaves her to it. She knows the Marrieds' eyes are all on her again. She looks up and stares at the woman opposite who manages a weak smile before burying her head in a magazine. She glances around the room again. They'd say it was her own fault even if they knew the truth.

When the sucking stops, Barbara looks down and sees that it's asleep. She puts it back in the cot and covers it with the yellow, crocheted blanket her mum brought in yesterday. She wipes herself clean and fastens her bra. Her Mum would be coming back with *him* today. She wouldn't believe her either.

Barbara gets out of bed and grabs some clothes from the locker. She takes a last look at the child, at the window and the bright blue sky, before walking through the ward doors, letting them swing closed behind her.

8 HIDDEN TREASURE

2015

'That's where it happened. Down there,' I say, pointing to where the waves are smashing against the rocks far below us. The seagulls are riding the currents and screaming at us...'*Fall...Fall...Fall*'. It reminds me of that day.

Charlie staggers back from the edge. One puff of wind could drag him over; he's such a weed.

'No chance,' he says. 'I'm not going down there.'

'You are. Even if I have to drag you.' He has to come with me. Wayne Jones is dead and I'm going to make the most of it, but I can't face it on my own.

Charlie whines again. 'I can't. You know I'm scared of heights. Can't we just go home?'

'God, you're a right wimp,' I say. 'It's no wonder they pick on you at school.'

'There were three of them. I didn't think it would be like this at big school. Why didn't you help me?'

I lean into his face. 'You've got to fight your own battles. I've managed to get to Year Twelve without anyone coming near me.'

Charlie's voice gets higher, snapping at me like a little dog.

'You're twice as big as me... Besides, you're in Wayne Jones's gang. Everyone's scared of him.'

'They won't be now he's dead. Let's get going.' I grab his arm and drag him back to the rim. 'There's a fortune down there and we're going to get it.'

'Please Neil, let's go home. I'll tell Dad. You wouldn't do it if he were here.'

He always has to bring Dad in to fight his battles. I dig my fingers deeper and he whimpers. When I push my face right up to his, his stupid, babyish, blue eyes and ginger hair are all I can see. I grit my teeth and spit the words out, spraying his face. 'One word and you're dead. Understand?' He nods his head frantically, like the dog in Mum's car. 'This is my chance to make some money and get away from this dump.'

'Okay...okay. You're hurting me.'

I let go, pushing him away, ignoring his tears. 'Right. Climb down to the first ledge and I'll follow you.' He's shaking like a lump of jelly as he lowers himself down, desperately trying to find a decent foothold. The chalky soil breaks away each time he puts any weight on it. 'Get on with it. You're worse than useless.'

'Dad says it's you that's useless,' he snaps. 'I-I can't reach it. Aaargh!'

His foot slips and he lands in a heap on the narrow ledge. Serves him right. Soft Git. I shin down the cliff face in less than a minute and join him. 'It's a good job there's a path from here. The tide'll be in before we get down there at this rate. Get up and stop snivelling.'

Charlie gets up slowly, rubbing his elbow. He follows me down the narrow path, spouting his usual tripe.

'If we were at home, you'd have got a right slap by now.'

'Yeah. Mustn't hurt Daddy's little soldier, must we? Just zip it.' I race down the path without stopping. When I reach the bottom, I look back to find he's barely halfway. 'C'mon, Snail. Move it.'

'Stop calling me Snail. I'm coming,' he shouts in his weedy voice.

He's not looking down to where the steep slope

drops away into thin air. I watch him leaning into the cliff side, grabbing the tussocks of grass for support as he tries to go faster. It brings it all back. I can still see Wayne slipping down the bank and disappearing over the side. I let the sounds of the sea and the seagulls fill my ears; block out the memory of his screams. 'About bloody time,' I say when Charlie finally reaches me and looks at the six-foot drop down to the beach. I point about fifty metres up the shoreline. 'There's the cave. The tide's already coming in so we'd best get a move on.' I jump down and my ankle twists over when I slide through the loose pebbles. 'Oh shit!' The pain shoots up my leg, making my eyes water. Charlie's eyes look ready to pop out as he sees what's happened to me.

'No chance. It's way too far.' he says.

I rub my ankle, sucking my breath in, trying not to cry out. 'Get your arse down here, or I'll come back up and push you over.'

'The tides coming in really fast. Y-you, go. It'll be quicker. I'll pull you back up when you come out.'

When I look down, the water's beginning to creep around my trainers. Glaring back up at him and over to the cave, I realise he's right. The last thing I need is him slowing me down. 'Stay put. I mean it, Snail. Move an inch and you're dead. Got it?'

'Yes, I've got it,' he mumbles as I hobble up the beach.

HOME TRUTHS

It hurts like hell every time I take a step. When I look back, Charlie's lying on his back with his legs dangling over the drop. He'd better be there when I get back.

After what seems like forever, I reach the entrance to the cave. The water's covering my trainers now, but the cold is helping to numb the pain in my foot. The tide's coming in quite fast and I speed up, half running, half limping until I reach the broad, flat, slab of rock where Wayne and I were going to come for the stash. Gritting my teeth, I place my hands on the edge and hoist myself up high on to the large stone platform. I peer up through the dark, to the shelf where we hid it. Another painful climb. When I get there, I grasp the bag and climb down again. Sitting on the cold slab for a while, I think about how my life will change. The pills are my passport out of here. I can leave home as soon as I've sold them. They can all go jump. No more having *him* on my case. No more listening to Mum saying it's my own fault for cheeking him. No more Snail snitching and getting me into trouble. Sliding the bag into my pocket, I stand up ready to start back. When I see the water already slapping against the side of the ledge, the panic rises and I shout as loud as I can. 'Charlie. Charlie.' There's no answer. He can't hear me from here. I'm stuck.

I wait a while and try again, cupping my hands around my mouth. 'Charlie.'

'What's up?'

He's standing at the cave entrance, his silhouette clear against the bright opening. Phew. He must have decided to come looking for me. He waves, beckoning me to come.

'Hurry up, the tide's coming in fast.'

'I can't, Charlie. You come here.'

'No chance.'

'Do it, you little creep.'

'Not if you call me a creep.'

'I mean it. You'd better get over here now.'

'Why should I? You'll only give me a belt if I do. I'm going home.'

'No! Charlie! Charlie! Please.'

'Why do you need me to come?' he yells again.

'I just do...I'll make it worth your while.' There's no way I'll let him know I'm scared.

'How much?'

'Half of whatever I get. Anything. Get over here now!'

'Promise? Anything I want?'

'Charlie, please. The tide's getting higher.'

'Okay, but you'd better keep your promise.'

He disappears as he comes further into the dark cave. I can hear him huffing and puffing his way towards me. 'About time.' I say as he comes into view.

'Give us your hand, then,' he says reaching out to me.

I pull him up. 'You took your time.'

'You'll keep your promise, won't you? Give me whatever I want?' he says, trying to stop his teeth chattering. His school trousers are stuck to his legs.

'Yeah, course. When we get out.'

'Is the fortune too heavy for you to carry on your own? Where is it? Show me!'

I put my hand in my pocket and pull out the bag.

'What's that? Drugs? You can't get mixed up with drugs you idiot. Chuck them away!'

I give him a backhanded slap in a flash. 'Don't call me an idiot! They're worth thousands.'

He rubs his shoulder. 'You must be mad? Why didn't you wade out before it got so deep?'

'Ankle hurts.'

'*Oh poor Neil,*' he says, mimicking the way I usually speak to him when I want to wind him up. 'It'll be okay if you swim.'

'Course it won't you idiot. Can't kick if it hurts can I?'

'Shame,' he says and stands up. 'You'll just have to put up with it. I'm going home.'

I grab his leg. 'No! No! Sorry...Don't go.'

'Sorry? Sorry and Please all on the same day?' He grins down at me. I could kill him, but I'm so scared of him leaving me. 'Alright, but you'd better stop having a go at me all the time.'

'I...I...It's my ankle. I think I've broken it.'

'No way. You wouldn't have been able to walk over here.'

'It's broken, I said. I should know, shouldn't I? Prat.'

He snatches his leg out of my grasp. 'Right, that's it. Get yourself out!'

I sound like a little kid when my voice comes out all whiny. 'Charlie. I'm sorry. Please, Charlie. Don't leave me.' I wipe my eyes with the sleeve of my shirt.

He sits down again. 'Neil? What is it?' He actually sounds concerned. 'I've never heard you cry before. Not even when Dad lays into you.'

'I can't swim.' I sob, ashamed of myself, burying my head in my hands.

He's surprised. 'You must have had lessons? Dad's always gone on about how important it is?'

'Only for you,' I snap. 'You always get everything you want.'

'If you weren't always giving him a load of backchat he might have taken you too.'

'He wouldn't. He's never liked me since the day he moved in.' My voice cracks and I turn away, blinking hard.

'He's your Dad. Of course, he likes...what do you mean *Moved in?*'

I turn back. 'When he moved in with Mum and me.'

'What are you on about?' he asks, frowning.

Haven't you sussed it yet? Look at me.' I tug on my thick, black mop. 'Ben's *your* Dad, Charlie. Not mine. My dad's dead.'

As soon as I say it his face changes. It's as if a light has switched on.

'S'pose. The dark hair and all that. But I've never really thought about it like that.'

'What?'

'You've always been my spiteful, big brother.' He smiled and put an arm around my shoulders. 'C'mon Neil. Dad loves you. If you'd stop kicking off all the time he'd...you never give him a chance to be nice.'

'I didn't like him at first. Didn't want him taking Dad's place. He doesn't care about me. He said he hadn't planned on bringing up someone else's kid either, but we'd both better get used to the idea.

'How old—'

'Five. He'd moved down here from someplace called Blackdale, up north. Mum says he has issues because his mum dumped him at birth. He was brought up by his grandparents. She says his grandad used to knock him about. Doesn't make it right for him to do the same to me.' I shrug his arm away.

'We've got to go, Neil. Now! The water's getting deeper. It'll be too late soon.'

'I can't, Charlie. I'm scared.'

'Scared? C'mon. I'll help you.' He sounds so calm. The water is wild. It's smashing against the cave walls. Neil holds his hand out. 'It's still shallow enough to wade if we go now.'

'You're sure?'

'Yes. Now move it.' He lowers himself into the water, pulling me with him. We both gasp as the cold hits. It's right up to his armpits, waist deep on me. 'Keep hold of my hand and follow me,' he said.

Staying close to the cave wall, we try to push our way through the water. A wave hits us hard, sweeps us along. 'I can't do this, Charlie.'

'We'll soon be out. Just keep hold of me.' He squeezes my hand. I can barely stay upright, yanking him back all the time. I'm blubbing like a baby. We could drown.

The roar of the waves gets louder and louder. As we reach the exit of the cave, the wind slams at us, forcing us back. The spray and froth pelts our faces. It's so hard to see. I'm screaming at him. 'We're going to die. Oh my God, we're going to die.' I let go of his hand and try to walk back inside the cave.

'Neil. Neil. Stop!' He reaches out to grab me and we both fall and go under.

I can't see Charlie as I bob up. Can't get my footing. A wave drags me under. Water in my mouth, my eyes, I can't see. My heart bangs as I try to hold my breath. Blood roars in my ears. I'm going to die. My arms reach out in all directions, trying to find something to grab. Nothing. The sea is pushing me back into the cave. I can't fight it. I stop struggling. I can't breathe. I'm sorry Charlie...I'm sorry...

*

Something's hammering on my chest. A gurgling sound. A moan. It's me. I'm choking. I splutter and gasp for air. Charlie's turning me onto my side and I vomit, coughing up water. My lungs are on fire.

'It's alright. You're alright, Neil.' I can hear him crying. 'You're alive. Thank God. You're alive.'

I try to speak but I can't. It hurts to breathe. Everything goes black.

When I come to, Charlie is kneeling over me. We're back on the stone platform. I try to sit up. 'Don't move,' he says. 'Stop and rest for a bit.'

'How?'

'I pulled you out.'

'But?'

'CPR. I learned at swimming lessons.'

It's so cold I'm shaking. The water's lapping the brim of the slab. 'You need to go,' I say.

'Not without you,' he says, shivering so much his teeth chatter.

Charlie stands up. He's looking all around the cave. 'When you used to come down with Wayne, did you bring torches?'

'Yeah, but we didn't leave them down here.'

'Are there any ledges higher up?' he asks.

'Only the one where we kept the stash so no-one would find it.'

'Great. How wide is it?' He sounds excited. 'If we can get higher up we'll be okay.'

'Doubt it. I don't think it'll hold our weight.'

'Where is it?' he asks, looking up into the dark.

'It's straight up from here, but you won't be able to climb up. Heights. Remember?' I don't want him to get hurt. 'I'm so sorry for dragging you down here, Charlie.'

He grins and scratches his chin. 'Mmm. Live... or die because you're scared of heights Charlie? What shall I do?' I force a laugh and he pats my shoulder. 'Can you give me a leg up? I'll try my weight first.'

I struggle to my feet. My legs are wobbly, the pain in my ankle makes me limp. I can hear the wheeze in my chest when I breathe. He waits until I've finished coughing. My throat burns like crazy.

I cup my hands and he pushes himself up, feeling for his first handhold. 'There are lots of places for your feet and hands,' I say.

It doesn't take him long to find the ledge. 'It's not

very deep, but it's wide enough for two of us. If something heavy falls on your head in a minute, don't worry it's only me.' I laugh and peer up at him. He shouts down again 'One...Two...Three. Well, it's holding me. Your turn.'

'I don't think I can manage it, Charlie.'

'Do you want me to call you a Wimp? Get your arse up here, or I'll give you something to snivel about.'

I laugh between coughs, half choking, at the thought of him bossing me about. 'Just you wait, Snail. You'll be sorry when I get up there.' I manage to cough and grunt my way up. He helps me to clear the rim and I'm soon sitting beside him.

'What took you so long?' he says. I can just about make out he's grinning in the gloom.

'Don't push it, Snail.'

'Hug me.'

'You what?' Now he's really gone too far. 'In your dreams, I'm not your mother.'

'We need to try and stay warm, so we don't get hypothermia.' He holds his arms out and shuffles up close. 'We'll be here for a long time.'

'Oh. I thought you were getting a bit, Lovey Dovey. Can't be having that.' He chuckles as I wrap my arms around him and rest my chin on his neck.

'Do you miss your real dad?' he asks.

'Never knew him. Mum says he died before I was born. Car crash.'

'I'm sorry. That's bad.'

'Not really. I was used to it being just Mum and me. Until—'

Charlie interrupts. 'What happened to Wayne?'

'He slipped.'

'Oh my God, Neil! Where?'

'On the path...I'd gone first and...and he pushed me out of his way. Said he was in charge. He tripped and lost his footing. I was scared of him, hated what he got me into, I never wished him dead though. Christ Charlie.' It feels like a stone's lodged in my throat and I can't swallow. 'It could have happened to you. I'm so...so...sorry.'

'Hey. Quit bawling. You're wetting my neck.' he mumbles, squeezing me.

We sit there holding on, his hand patting my back, mine patting his.

'Now it's time to keep your promise,' he says, his warm breath tickling my ear.

'Can't do that before I've sold them,' I say, sitting back and pulling the plastic bag from my pocket. I check they are still dry. They are.

'Yes, you can. You said I could have anything I wanted.'

What's he looking so worried for? 'You don't want half the money?'

'No.'

'Cool. Thanks, Charlie,' I can't believe my luck. 'What *do* you want?'

'Two things.'

'Okay,' I say, shuffling around and wondering what he's going to ask for.

'Promise?'

'Promise.'

'Cross your heart?'

'Cross my heart.' I cross my heart with my finger. 'For God's sake. Get on with it.'

'Alright. Keep your hair on. One...Throw the pills into the sea.'

'What? You must-'

'Two... Come home and teach me how to stand up for myself.'

9 THE KEY TO FREEDOM

2016

We wandered back through the small Bulgarian town of Balchik on the Black Sea, my annoyingly pale skin pricking with the unaccustomed heat. The little, whitewashed houses with red tiled roofs clung to the chalky hillsides in the late afternoon sun. It felt good to get away on our first real holiday together even though it was only for a week during half term. I still found it hard to trust anyone, but Jack had been patient and kind. Maybe this holiday would wash away any reservations I still had.

The tangy smell of the sea mingled with the rich aromas drifting from the local restaurants as we eyed the menus outside, trying to decide where to have dinner that evening.

'This one looks nice, Melanie. It's all seafood and there's a roof terrace. We'll get a good view from up there. What do you think?' Jack shielded his dark brown eyes and squinted, tipping his head of black curls to look up at the trailing vines and the tops of red sun umbrellas. He was already deeply tanned and his T-shirt was tight over his beautifully toned torso.

'Fine, as long as you like it,' I said.

He looked at me. I knew he wanted to say something about my comment, but he forced a smile and said, 'C'mon, I'll race you back to the villa.'

I grinned and set off at speed, holding my straw sunhat down. My copper plait swung out behind me, slapping each red shoulder in turn. As a P.E. teacher, Jack was far fitter than me. Being a primary school teacher didn't usually involve too much strenuous exercise.

He glanced back at me. 'You can't be flagging already,' he said and laughed loudly, but as he reached the gate, he stopped abruptly and stared at something. 'Bloody Hell!'

I slowed down to catch my breath. That's when I saw her. A young woman was lying on the ground in front of the double garage doors. She was clutching a small brass key and appeared to be asleep when I approached. Her dark hair was short and matted to her skull. Her clothes were filthy and torn, and a cloying, sickly smell emanated like a thick blanket around her. I stepped back and retched. The girl was desperately thin, her skin contouring her skeleton like cling film. The sight made me shudder. She opened her large, sunken black eyes and stared at me.

'Molia. Moje li a mi pomognete?' she whispered.

I dropped to my knees 'I'm sorry. I don't speak Bulgarian.'

I tried to help her sit up, but she whimpered when I touched her. Jack stood over us, the back of his hand over his mouth. He looked down at me and squeezed my shoulder reassuringly.

Picking the girl up in his arms took such a long time, as every bone seemed to protrude, threatening to tear her skin and burst through. His tenderness towards her touched me deeply.

'I've carried babies that weigh more than this,' he commented, then carried her up the external stairs than ran up the outside of the garage wall, through the door and into the enormous open plan living area and kitchen space. It covered the whole of the first floor in the brand new villa.

Jack laid the girl down, as gently as possible, on one of the brown leather sofas and brought her a glass of water. She gulped it down, spilling most of it.

I rifled through the drawers in an oak bureau, pulling out the list of 'important numbers' we had found in the welcome pack on arrival. 'Lekar' was at the top of the list. I tapped out the number on my mobile.

'Ne! Ne!' The girl stretched out her hand.

'I'm only ringing for the doctor. Lekar,' I said. 'You need help.'

'Ne. Molia. Ne.' her faced screwed up as tears cut lines through the dirt on her face.

I looked at Jack for inspiration, wiping my own eyes fiercely.

'Don't be daft, Melanie. We've got to call a doctor. The police'll need to know as well. We've no idea what lunatic did this to her - and he could come looking.' Jack took his own mobile out of his pocket.

'Please! Can we wait and try and find out who she is first? She's frightened and I know how that feels.'

'No. We have to do the right thing. Look at her!' He waved his hand towards, Anya. 'She needs help.'

Surely, he must understand? 'You gave me time when I needed help...'

Jack stared at me and then the girl.

'Please?'

Jack sighed, shrugging his shoulders. He was shaking his head as he headed into the kitchen.

I turned to Anya. 'Can I get you something to eat?' I asked, holding my fingers up to my mouth.

'Da. Da.'

'We're ringing for a doctor after she's eaten,' Jack said firmly as he returned a few minutes later, carrying a plate of food.

The girl inhaled the smell of the local honey and buttered bread before cramming it into her mouth, not waiting to swallow before the next handful followed. It wasn't long before she vomited all over the brown tiled floor. I brought her another glass of water.

'I'm Melanie and this is Jack. See!' I said, pointing to each of us in turn. 'Melanie...Jack. You? What's your name?'

'Anya.'

'Now then, Anya. Where do you belong?' Jack asked. Her face was blank.

I asked her if she would like to wash, miming the act so she could understand. Even though the doors leading out to the balcony were wide open, the smell from her was still overpowering.

Anya looked around, her eyes darting into every corner.

Jack held out his arms, offering to carry her again but she shrank back into the sofa. He waited patiently, smiling at her. 'I'll be gentle,' he said.

She swallowed hard and nodded. Jack cradled her and carried her upstairs to the bathroom on the second floor. Sitting her down on a chair next to the roll top bath, he left us while I ran the water and poured in my own scented bath gel. I undressed her slowly. Her body was filthy, but I could still make out the half-healed sores and the purple bruising on almost every part of her. Who had done this? I couldn't halt the tears as I helped Anya into the warm water. Was I crying for her or both of us? The times I had sought comfort in a warm bath came back to me. She tensed her body and cried out at first but eventually slid through the bubbles and relaxed. Thoughts of my ex-husband filled my own body with remembered pain.

Anya looked at me and took my hand. 'Vie ste mnogo mil,' she whispered.

I felt gratitude and understanding in her touch. Could she sense my own suffering? No one had ever suspected the local MP of abuse. "Such a nice man" they always said.

*

Anya was propped up on the sofa with pillows. I spoon fed her thick meat soup I had made from leftovers in the fridge. She was smiling and kept touching the white cotton t-shirt that hung like a dress on her tiny frame. It looked like an oversized shroud. Jack held up the small brass key.

Anya flung her arms wide and then pointed to the floor.

'This house?' From his pocket, he pulled out the set of barrel lock keys we had been given on arrival. 'No. Not here. It wouldn't fit the lock.'

Anya frowned. 'Ne. Ne.' She shook her head and flung her arms wide again, pointing to the floor. We didn't understand.

I fetched a local tourist map of Bulgaria. She pointed to Balchik. 'Baba,' she said. Her eyes continued to scour the map until her finger finally settled on a place far to the west of where they were. 'Anya. Skopje... Monopol... Tabac.' She made a walking action with her fingers across the paper.

'You walked here from Skopje?'

'Da. Da. Baba.'

She pointed to herself. 'Anya, Evrein.' The tears fell again. 'Tato, Mamo, murtov. Ne Lekar. Ne Politsiya.'

'No Doctor. No Police. I promise.' I couldn't betray her trust.

'Aye, well. We'll see in the morning.' said Jack, frowning at me.

He carried her upstairs again and laid her down on one of the twin beds in the second bedroom.

'Anya! Anya!' she said, pointing at herself again.

'I know you're Anya.' I said kissing her forehead. 'It's okay now. No one is going to hurt you anymore. I'll look after you.'

'Mnogo. Mnogo.' She drifted into sleep while holding my hand. Finally, peaceful.

*

1943

The Herz family clung to each other. Along with hundreds more, they were waiting to be loaded onto a train for Treblinka. Even the disgusting conditions they had tolerated for the last two years in the tobacco warehouse here at Skopje must be better than what they had heard about Treblinka. It was nicknamed the 'Death Camp' by their German guards.

The guards shouted commands at the crowd, herding them, like the cattle that were usually transported this way, onto the freight train. Parents were screaming as their children became separated from them, crying as they were bullied and pushed up into the waiting wagons without their loved ones.

A woman fell and was trampled in the crush. Her husband tried in vain to lift her up again. He was beaten over the head with a pistol for his trouble and dragged away from the platform. The guard made the man kneel down before he held the gun to the back of his head and pulled the trigger. The guard went back to his duties as if nothing had happened as the train whistle blew. People scrambled on board in a panic.

Tato and Mamo were speaking to Anya in whispers as they inched forward, hoping the guards couldn't understand their local Bulgarian tongue.

Tato tried to hide his tears as he squeezed her shoulders. 'When I say NOW, you must run as fast as you can across the field to the woods, Anya. Don't stop. Whatever happens, don't stop. Head east and keep going. The sun rises in the east. Go to Baba. Promise me.'

Anya nodded, desperate not to show them how scared she was. At sixteen, she understood the danger they were in.

More families had joined them in the race for freedom. Anya had to keep running as Tato said, the sound of gunfire rattling in her ears. People were falling like stones all around her. She knew that Mamo and Tato had been shot when she made it into the forest and looked back. A field of scattered bodies, some moaning, some absolutely still, lay before her. She wanted to scream for her parents, to go back and look for them. There was no one else in the wood. She realised she was the only survivor as she turned away.

She started to run. She kept on running until she was blinded by her tears, running until the stitch in her side was too painful, running until she could run no more and finally dropped to her knees. Her lungs hurt so much she could hardly breathe. All she could hear were her own gasps for breath and the thudding noise in her temples. When her heart rate slowed down, she listened for any sounds and was comforted by the silence. She covered herself with leaves and lay there for two days, too terrified to cry or move, even though the cold was unbearable. She wished herself dead so she could be with her parents again. On the third day, desperate thirst and hunger pains made her move.

She didn't have much idea of where she was, but she remembered what Tato had said about the sun. Starting out each night just as the sun was setting behind her; it took over a week to reach the Bulgarian border. There was still a long way to go. She survived by stealing eggs from farms, sleeping during the day in ditches and woodland and if she was lucky, she found a deserted barn. She ate anything she could find: pig slop, rotten potatoes, chicken feed. She avoided big towns and cities. It seemed safer in the country where she was less likely to run into soldiers. The thought of Baba drove her on, day after day. She needed to let her know what had happened to Tato and Mamo. Wild flowers created a patchwork of colour in the meadows and apple blossom dressed the trees before dancing away like tiny pink butterflies in the breeze. It brought back memories of living in Balchik with Tato, Mamo, Uncle Jacob and Baba.

It was a small cottage near the sea; perched high on a hillside where they kept goats and a few chickens. Mamo grew vegetables, which she and Anya would take, along with any surplus eggs, to the market each week to sell. Baba made the most beautiful bread in the world. She longed for the smell and taste again.

When the soldiers came to take them away, they didn't see Baba and Uncle Jacob hiding in the goat pen. Anya and her parents were loaded into open-topped Lorries along with every other Jew in the town. She had sobbed as the place she had known as home for the last fourteen years disappeared in a cloud of dust behind the convoy.

She pushed on and counted off the days by making marks on her arm. Anya guessed it was early June when she finally came to the small village she had been longing to see. She tried to stay hidden as she stumbled up the familiar hill.

The cottage wasn't there. Only a pile of rubble welcomed her. Scrambling through the heap of stones trying to find something recognisable, she spotted a piece of pottery. It was Baba's pot, the one she always used when making Kavarm. She could smell the wonderful meat stew. What she wouldn't give for a bowl now. That's when she saw the key: Baba's key. Holding it tightly in her hand as she lay amongst the dirt and stone, her mind drifted and she imagined herself sitting at the table. Baba was laughing and everyone was so happy. Tato and Mamo were there. 'I thought you were dead.' Anya whispered as the light faded and she closed her eyes.

She remembered hearing engine noises and voices. 'It's Anya. I'm here.' she cried, but no one heard.

The darkness came again. She awoke after what seemed like an eternity to find two people in strange clothes staring down at her.

*

2016

Jack and I sat down on the sofa with a glass of wine. The awful smell still lingered.

'It's so awful. Who did this to her?' I cried, snuggling into his arms.

'I dunno. I'll land one on him if he comes back though. Now dry your eyes and help me find out who she is.'

He opened his laptop and googled, 'Skopje Monopol Tabac'. A photo appeared of a woman standing in front of a plaque set in a wall. Flowers and wreaths covered the ground in front of it. The Headline read:

'MACEDONIA REMEMBERS TINY JEWISH COMMUNITY'.

A woman stands in front of a memorial for 7,144 Macedonian Jews, in the MONOPOLY TOBACCO WAREHOUSES in Skopje, Macedonia, on Monday, March 11, 2013.

Macedonia commemorates 70-years of the holocaust of its Jewish community, almost completely wiped out during the Nazis' occupation of this tiny Balkan country during World War II.

'I don't understand,' I said, my eyes wide. 'Is this where she walked from?'

Jack keyed 'Baba', into Google Translate. 'Grandmother. She was here to see her Gran. Poor lass. She's walked hundreds of miles. It must have taken weeks to get here. It was her Gran's key she was holding.'

'No wonder she was confused about where she was. She thought this was her Gran's!'

*

It was early the next morning when Jack and I crept downstairs. We didn't disturb Anya.

'We'll let her sleep a bit,' Jack said, smiling at me.

'I'll get a doctor when she wakes up.'

We ate breakfast on the balcony, looking down at the town and the turquoise sea beyond. There was an aura of peace but... something was different. I couldn't identify what it was. The sky was gloriously blue and the temperature was already over twenty-five degrees. Jack pulled out the laptop again.

'Anya's Jewish, Melanie. Evrein means Jew.'

I went back inside to get the telephone number of the people who owned the villa. They might know where Anya's grandmother was living now.

From the back of a drawer in the bureau, I pulled out a pamphlet I hadn't taken any interest in before. It contained photographs and the story of when and how the villa had been built.

I couldn't believe what I was reading. I went back outside to find Jack. 'Listen to this. It's crazy...

The owner's, Isaac and Judith Herz, inherited the small cottage and land a couple of years ago. It hadn't been lived in for seventy years, not since Isaac's great-grandmother, Rachel and her son, Jacob (Isaac's grandfather) fled after the Germans rounded up the rest of their family. They were shipped off to Skopje, where they were imprisoned in the tobacco warehouses until being transported to Treblinka in 1943.

Isaac and Judith built the existing villa and this is their first year of letting it out. During the clearing of the site, the workmen found the skeleton of a young girl who held a key within the fragile finger bones of her left hand.'

I paused to look at Jack, my mouth trembling as I continued...

'The authorities and experts were called in and it was determined she must have been there for at least sixty years or more. Isaac and Judith organised a service and buried her in the garden as a mark of respect, but no one has any idea of who she might have been.'

My eyes clouded with tears as they rested on a family photo, printed onto the bottom of the sheet. Its header said that it had been taken outside the cottage in 1940. I traced the outline of a young girl who was smiling into the camera. 'How can Anya be this girl in the photo?'

'Don't be silly.' Jack looked over my shoulder at the photograph. 'Good grief!'

'Do you think it's her grandmother?' I asked. I couldn't get my head around it.

'It's the spitting image.'

I turned the sheet of paper over and found the list

of names. 'Oh! It is Anya. I don't understand.'

We both looked up the stairs.

'I don't understand it either but, wherever she's been, she's free now.' Jack said and put his arm around my shoulder.

The words echoed in my head. I'm free too, I thought. Finally free to be me and love Jack the way he deserves. The way I know he loves me. I squeezed his hand.

I realised the 'something different' was the smell. It had gone and, glancing upstairs again, I knew she had gone too. I passed the pamphlet to Jack and went to look for the grave that needed a name.

10 NURSING A GRUDGE

2017

The half-eaten Gerry Giraffe birthday cake with its five candles was still sitting on the breakfast bar, alongside the matching paper party plates and sandwich crusts. Sam had wanted to have the party up at Blackdale Golf Club, but Ruth was on nights and couldn't get the time off. It was all she could do to survive on the few hours' sleep she snatched during the day. The sound of a distant lawnmower drifted through the open kitchen window. Ruth looked out onto the well-tended garden where Sam was on his knees. Olivia, still wearing her pointed, pink party hat, was sitting on the grass beside him.

Ruth brushed her pale-blue uniform down, pinned on her pocket watch and leaned over the worktop. She pushed the window open a little wider. 'I'm off now. Have a lovely evening.'

Sam flipped a hand in acknowledgement. He was mending a trellis that formed part of a pergola. The fragile latticework, which supported the Nellie Moser Clematis was falling apart after a few severe winters.

'Pass me another tack please, Olivia.' Sam combed his long fingers through his thick dark-brown hair and grinned at his daughter.

'Careful with my flowers, Daddy.' Olivia picked up a blousy pink flower head that had fallen on the grass. At five years old her soft hazel eyes and crown of cinnamon curls revealed a mini replica of her mother, except for the wide-open smile capable of melting ice. That definitely came from Sam.

'Sorry, Princess. I'll try to be gentler,' he said, stroking her cheek and putting on his 'sad' face.

'It's okay, Daddy,' she answered and kissed him on the nose.

As usual, they were both too engrossed in their own little world to pay Ruth any attention. She tried again, calling through the gap in the window, this time a little louder.

'I should be home early enough to give Olivia her breakfast and take her to school.'

'Let's hope there won't be any emergencies then.' he replied, still not looking at her.

'I'll just tell all the patients not to be ill, shall I?' she threw back at him.

Olivia blew her a kiss. 'Bye, Mummy. Love you.'

'I love you too sweetheart,' Ruth said, smiling. She blew a kiss back to her daughter.

Turning away, she picked up her car keys and headed for the door.

*

'Mr Carter's eaten well today. His obs are fine, so he should be going home tomorrow. Moving in with his son...poor thing...won't be able to sneeze without an inquisition.'

'I know. Still, it's better than not being wanted at all.' said Ruth, perched on the corner of the desk as Sally started the handover. The nurse's station was facing the open double doors of the ward, so it was easy to keep an eye on all the patients. The lights in this area had been dimmed to aid rest, but a work lamp provided a halo of light over the paperwork.

'Too right. We can't trace any relatives for Mr Freeman. He's had another small stroke. We've upped the medication. Seems to be responding positively. Katie's with him now,' she added, nodding in the direction of Mr Freeman's bed.

'Such a shame.' Ruth had warmed to his gentle nature. He never complained about anything.

'There's a new patient in the private room: Rufus

Downs, seventy-five, not expected to last the night. Cancer. Gracie, his daughter...'

Ruth had stopped listening.

'Ruth. Ruth? Are you okay? You look a bit pale. Come and sit down.' Sally manoeuvred her into a chair. 'Are you ill?'

'S...sorry, Sal. I'm fine. Fine. What were you saying?'

'I was saying, Rufus Downs, his daughter is sitting with him. She's quite distraught. Keeps calling us in every few minutes. We've put him on a syringe driver for the pain. He's refusing food, but he's on a drip for fluids. Are you sure you're alright? '

'Yes. Of course.' Ruth stood up and took the patient files from Sally.

'If you're sure?' Sally wasn't convinced. 'That's about it, everyone else the same, no changes. I've been through everything with Katie. Jenny hasn't arrived yet. You really don't look very well.' Sally frowned. 'Is it Sam? Still giving you a hard time?'

Ruth took a deep breath, choosing her words carefully. 'Only the usual. He hates me being on nights. Thinks I don't spend enough time with him and Olivia.'

'Flaming dinosaur that's what. He knows how important this job is to you. Try not to worry. He'll come round.' She put her coat on and picked up her bag. Heading up the corridor, she turned back and added. 'We'll catch up in the morning. Plan the weekend.' Sally wasn't convinced that Ruth had told her everything but there was little she could do. She would tell her what else was bothering her in her own good time. She always did.

'What? Yes. You get off. See you in the morning.' Ruth stared over at the private ward door again and saw Jenny racing up the corridor towards her.

'Sorry I'm late, couldn't get the dog to have a poo before I locked him in for the night,' Jenny's voice was hoarse from running as she threw her coat off and hung it up. 'Anything I need to know?'

*

Ruth started her patient rounds, heading to Mr Carter first. Her mind was in a whirl. She hadn't heard Rufus's name spoken aloud for over thirty-five years. Not since her mother had wiped him from their lives. She'd been the same age as Olivia is now. There couldn't be another one. It must be him.

Ruth held Mr Carter's wrist. She could feel the delicate pulse through his finely veined skin. He reminded her of what a Grandpa should look like. His shiny pink head, mottled with age spots, was bald on top. A wide strip of white hair started from just above his left ear, skirted around the back of his crown and finished at his right ear. His thick white moustache and laughing, blue eyes completed the picture. 'It'll be nice to live with your son, won't it, Mr Carter?'

'I'd rather live with you, Ruth. I'd die a happy man if I had you to look at every day.' He chuckled.

'Now you behave yourself. You'll have my Sam after you,' she replied, forcing a laugh and wagging her finger at him playfully. Not much hope of that, she thought. He always seemed on the verge of walking out these days. She glanced over at the door of the private room. Just like him. Her eyes clouded.

'Hey. You alright love? Something wrong?' Mr Carter's brow furrowed.

'Absolutely fine, Mr Carter. Now you settle down and get some sleep. Need you all nice and fresh to go home in the morning.' She squeezed his hand and continued to the next bed.

She heard someone shout, 'Nurse' and stopped in her tracks. She waited, not turning. *C'mon Jenny, Katie, anyone—answer her. I can't do it. Please*. No one responded. Ruth turned slowly, switching on a protective smile.

'I...I'll be with you as soon as I can.' She spoke slowly so as not to betray the pounding in her heart, before turning back and continuing up the ward. She couldn't simply run to him, could she? It wasn't fair on her other patients.

The daughter looked about the same age as herself? *Is that why he'd left?* Anger bubbled up inside as she made her way to each patient, checking temperatures, blood pressure, tucking them in, reassuring them wherever she sensed they were troubled, giving the time each one needed.

Eventually, when she could put it off no longer' she made her way to the private room. Straightening her uniform and brushing herself off outside the door, she put her best foot forward, knocked and marched in.

*

Gracie was sitting, hunched up and holding his hand, tears running down her pale freckled face. She looked up at Ruth, her glossy green eyes begging for someone to make everything alright. Her hair was slightly redder than Ruth's. More like paprika but the curls were just as wild.

Ruth forced herself to look away as she checked the drip.

'Everything seems fine,' she said hearing the choke in her own voice as her eyes looked down at the frail man lying there. His breathing weak and spasmodic, his chest heaving at the effort. Rufus Downs turned his head towards her, his eyes flickering open.

'Gracie? Is that you?' He peered at Ruth, unsure.

'No Dad. It's the nurse. She's come to make you comfortable.'

He was confused as his eyes turned to Gracie. Her hand was stroking his, trying to warm it.

Ruth picked up his other hand to check the pulse.

'Yes. I'm the nurse, Mr Downs.' She concurred with Gracie, but her eyes were firmly fixed on Rufus. 'Ruth. My name's Ruth.' Her voice was hard.

'Ruth? Ruth!' His head snapped her way again.

'Don't stare, Dad,' said Gracie. 'It's rude.' She managed a watery smile. 'I'm sorry Ruth. He gets a bit confused. He's in so much pain.' Her head dropped as she kissed his hand. Rufus stroked her hair, but his eyes never left Ruth's face.

'It's okay, Gracie,' he whispered. It's okay.'

'I need to go. I'll be back to check in a while,' mumbled Ruth as she hurried from the room.

*

Ruth slumped into the workstation chair. She attempted to write up her notes but was too upset and angry. All this time and now he was dying. She wouldn't ever get to know him. Gracie had known him all her life. Why hadn't he ever been back to see her? She was glad he was dying. Glad. She didn't need him. She'd tell Gracie what sort of a man he really was. She had a right to know. She...

'Nurse? Err? Ruth?'

Ruth realised her face was wet. She snatched the tears away before looking up.

'Can I help you?'

Ruth watched Gracie look around at the dimly lit ward, everything was quiet. She could probably see the other two nurses through the staff room door drinking coffee and chatting in whispers.

'I'm sorry to keep bothering you. It's...I don't know why but Dad keeps saying your name over and over. Would you mind coming in to reassure him for a minute? I know you're busy...'

'I'm coming.' Ruth said. She painted on a smile once more and followed Gracie.

Rufus looked so small and vulnerable. He wasn't the giant who had kissed her goodbye all those years ago. Saying how he would always love her. The band of steel tightened around her heart again.

'What's the matter, Mr Downs? Do you need the dosage upping?' she asked, walking over to the drip and adjusting the flow.

'Ruth—I need to tell you—'

'You don't need to tell me anything, Mr Downs.' interrupted Ruth. 'Your family is more important.' She pulled his wrist up and concentrated on her pocket watch, checking his pulse.

'Have *you* still got parents, Ruth?' Gracie asked quietly.

'No.' She glared at Rufus. 'No Gracie. My Mum died last year and my father...well, he left home when I was five years old. Found someone else he'd rather be with than Mum and me.'

'Oh, I'm so sorry. I've been so lucky. He's been a wonderful father. Haven't you Dad?' Gracie put her hands over her mouth. 'Sorry, Ruth that was tactless of me.'

'Not a problem. I'm sure he has. I wish I'd had a father like that.' She could see Rufus's eyes searching hers, rheumy and shining. Putting a thermometer in his ear, she went on. 'I wish he hadn't left my Mum crying herself to sleep every night. It left me wondering what I'd done wrong.' She wanted to scream at him. It was too much.

'Ruth...I'm sorry. I' his voice faltered, barely a whisper now.

'Typical of my Dad.' interrupted Gracie. 'He hates to see anyone hurt. You need to rest Dad. Don't talk anymore.'

'He's no need to worry about me. My father means nothing to me. Nothing!' said Ruth. She picked up the chart hanging from the end of the bed and scribbled down his observations.

Gracie stood up. 'I'm so sorry to be such a nuisance but would you mind very much if I went and got a coffee while you're here? I haven't had anything to drink or eat since we got here this afternoon.'

Ruth wasn't sure. She wasn't sure she could trust herself to be left alone with him but she had to stay professional.

'No problem. You get off. There's a cafe downstairs. He'll be fine.' Ruth couldn't help feeling a little sorry for her. It certainly wasn't Gracie's fault her father was a cheat and a liar.

After Gracie had gone, Ruth continued writing out the chart, her hand trembling. She could feel his eyes on her.

'She doesn't know,' he said.

'Obviously. Perhaps it's time she did.'

'I came back. Your Mum...she wouldn't—'

'Don't you dare blame Mum!' Ruth slammed the obs board back into its holder. 'You left us,' she snapped, her eyes flashing with anger.

'Please, Ruth. Gracie...it would—'

Ruth flew to the side of the bed and leaned over him. 'What? Show her what you're really like?'

Rufus gasped, struggling to breathe. 'I've no right to ask.' He held his hand out to her.

'That's correct. You have no right at all.' she snapped, ignoring the gesture. 'Why? Why did you leave? For her?' Ruth nodded towards the door.

'No. I met June...her Mum...after I left. There wasn't—' Rufus was overcome by a bout of coughing.

Ruth's tone softened, choked, her voice a whisper, as she tried to halt the tears. 'Then why? I thought you loved me?'

'I did! I do!' He mouthed between the rasping noises coming from his throat. 'Your mother didn't understand...my job. She said I thought... my job...too important...more important than her...you.' He couldn't catch his breath.

Ruth put her arm around him and raised him up, plumping his pillows. She poured some water and held it to his lips. 'You'd better stop talking now,' she said, putting the plastic cup down.

Gracie came in, holding a takeaway coffee in her hand. 'I didn't want to leave him for too long,' she said, looking from one to the other for a moment before sitting down. 'How has he been?'

'He's fine. Better now that you're back.' Ruth touched Gracie's shoulder and unsure of what else to say, left the room.

*

Ruth sat at her desk. Her head was spinning with everything that had happened tonight. She looked down the ward and saw Mr Carter's light was still on. She walked over to him.

'Everything okay?'

'I can't sleep.'

'What is it, Mr Carter?'

He shook his head, the loose skin under his chin wobbling. 'It won't work. With Tom, I mean.'

Ruth put her arm across his back and pushed him into a seated position while she rearranged his pillows. 'What won't work?'

'Living with him,' he said when she'd finished. 'We haven't exactly got a good track record.'

'Don't worry. Everyone has ups and downs. It'll be

fine. You'll see,' she said with a smile.

'I wish it were as simple as that.' He stroked the top of his head with his hand. It was...we had a massive fallout.'

Ruth couldn't help thinking about Rufus when he said this.

'He...he was only eighteen...left home. Didn't see him for years.'

Ruth touched his hand. 'You...You're okay now though, aren't you?'

'Well yes...he came back just before his mother died last year.' His eyes filled and he took a minute to steady himself. 'More to make peace with her than me, I think.' he leaned over and took a handkerchief from the drawer in his bedside cabinet. Wiping his eyes, he continued. 'We're trying...it's difficult.'

Ruth let go of his hand and stood up. 'Tell him how you feel. He'll understand. You're still his dad,' she said, stroking his arm.

'Not much of a dad, Ruth.' He shook his head from side to side. 'Too busy with my own life back then. Wish I'd done things differently.'

Ruth glanced over her shoulder at the closed door of the private ward. 'We can all wish that.' She gripped his hand with both of hers and shook it. 'Sort it out,

Fred. Before it's too late. I've got...I need to do something...'

Ruth half walked, half ran, back to her desk and picked up her mobile. Pausing for a minute, she searched her mind for the right words.

She keyed in a text message to Sam.

"Can you take the morning off? We need to sit down and talk about things. I miss you. Ruth xxx"

Gracie was standing in the doorway to Rufus's room and staring at her. 'I think he's gone.'

Ruth hurried over and put her arms around Gracie. She led her into the room, guiding her back to her seat.

*

Ruth lifted Rufus's wrist, feeling for a pulse.

'He's still here, Gracie, but he's frail.' said Ruth.

She had her back to Gracie but heard the audible gasp of anguish coming from her half-sister. Putting her fingers to her own lips first, Ruth pressed them to his forehead. While she stroked his face, his eyes flickered and opened. He tried to smile. His hand reached out and she took it, stroking it gently.

'He's not in pain, Gracie. He needs you to be strong for him now. Come and hold his hand.'

Gracie leaned over her father, her eyes puffed and red raw from crying. Her hands wringing the sodden handkerchief. He was near the end. Ruth took a deep breath and placed her hand on Gracie's shoulder.

'It's okay Gracie. He's so glad you're here. It means everything to him.'

She smiled. 'Thank you, Ruth. I'll be fine. We'll be fine.'

'I'll be right out there if you need me.' Ruth looked at her father one last time and left him to say goodbye to his daughter.

She saw the intermittent glow of her mobile amongst the papers on her desk. She sprinted over and rifled through all the documents on the desktop to find her phone.

She read the message from Sam.

"Missing you. Sxxx".

11 TAKING TIME OUT

1983

Why had she thought that coming back to her parents' house was a good idea? Louise wasn't the same person, no longer the girl who had left all those years ago. She was a stranger, an unknown guest they would have to endure for the weekend. She couldn't expect a warm welcome. Not after what she had done.

    Louise had got off the bus ten minutes ago but was still sitting on the cold, wooden bench. She pulled her thick, wool coat tighter. They ought to change the name. The last thing you could call this was a bus *shelter*. The wind rattled the glass panes behind her; fine rain blew in the open front and stung her face.

HOME TRUTHS

Checking her watch for the umpteenth time, she felt her pulse quicken as she remembered the sound of the ambulance leaving the photo shoot this morning. David, groaning and holding his side, shouting for her to follow on.

The rain stopped as suddenly as it had started and the setting sun cast an insipid yellow sheen on the late afternoon sky. She couldn't sit there all afternoon.

She stood up, clutching the collar of her coat to keep it close around her neck. She grabbed the handle of her suitcase and set off, wheeling it along the cracked paving stones. The tiny wheels rumbled and echoed over the old bridge and past the familiar cafe, thumping down the kerbs as she crossed each junction along the deserted, Sunday afternoon, roads of Blackdale. She passed street after street of terraced homes until she reached the simple, two up-two down, terraced house on Blake Street.

*

When her father opened the door, the sight of him in his home-knitted, sleeveless jersey and rolled shirtsleeves made her want to hug him close, but the hard look in his eyes as he stared at her in disbelief stopped her in her tracks.

'You'd better come in,' he said, eyeing her suitcase before leaving her standing there as he retreated to the front room. Louise, shaking, lifted her case over the threshold before putting it down in the hall and following him into the warmth. The lingering smell of roast beef and cabbage filled her nostrils, making her swallow the saliva bubbling up on her tongue.

'Hello Mum,' she said. Her mother looked up from the comfortable, fireside seat.

'Louise. Oh, Louise.' Alice jumped up and flung her arms around her daughter. 'You're back.'

Louise clung on to her mother, breathing her in, the familiar scent of 4711 telling her she was actually home.

'Come and sit by the fire. You must be frozen stiff,' her mother said as if Louise had just got back from popping to the shop.

Louise took off her coat and sat in the armchair her mother was offering. She stretched her hands out to the fire to warm them. 'It hasn't changed a bit,' she murmured.

'I'll put the kettle on and then you can tell me all your news,' her mum said. Her face was beaming as she scuttled out of the room.

Louise checked the time. Yes. Tea would be good.

Her father cleared his throat. 'You look well,' he said. She knew he was referring to the tailored suit she'd been wearing for the photo shoot this morning, rather than her. There hadn't been time to change. His voice sounded harsh, colder than she remembered. There was a slight hoarseness when he spoke.

'Thanks,' she said. 'and you?'

'Oh! You're interested, are you?'

Louise swallowed hard. 'Of course.' She didn't know what else to say. The silence spread, both of them feeling awkward. Their gaze was firmly fixed on the flames licking up the black back of the chimney, their attention on the coal as it cracked, split and shifted in the open hearth.

'Here we are.' Louise's mother spoke cheerily, briskly, as she came back into the room carrying a tray.

Louise's father sneered at his wife. 'Since when did we use cups and saucers and a teapot?' She watched her mother's face redden.

'I...I thought it would be...you know? What she's used to...'

Louise felt embarrassed for her. 'It's lovely Mum. Thank you.' She stood up and automatically retrieved the light, watermarked coffee table, from its home under the netted window and put it in front of the fire. Taking the tray, she signalled her mum to sit back down in her armchair. 'I'll be mother,' she said, smiling broadly.

'I noticed your suitcase in the hall. Are you stopping long?'

'Only until something better comes along,' her father said, glaring at her.

It felt like a slap and Louise's face was now the one turning pink. She didn't blame him for being angry. 'I...I was hoping to spend a couple of days. If that's okay?'

'Of course, love.' Her mother looked up at her. The china-blue eyes that had always been her best feature, now looked a dull grey to Louise, as if they had changed with age to match her hair colour. Louise turned away, tears pricking her own eyes as she poured the tea.

'Had enough of you has he?'

'Don't, George. She'll tell us when she's ready.'

'You're a right glutton for punishment, Alice.'

Louise passed the cups to her mum and dad, the china rattling in the saucers.

'Thank you, love,' said her mum. Her father took his from her without a word.

'Would you prefer it if I went?' she asked, her head cast down, unable to look directly at him.

'Do what you like! You always have.'

Louise poured herself some tea and sat on one of

the spindle-back chairs by the dining table. She looked at her watch. It had been one o'clock when she'd rung the hospital from a phone box at Kings Cross. They'd removed his appendix and he was sitting up and talking. He'd be counting the minutes. 'I've left, David. I couldn't...He was—'

'What? Too dull? Wouldn't let you walk all over him?'

'Stop it, George.' Alice glared at him, got to her feet and pulled up another dining chair. 'Give her a chance.' Facing her daughter and taking hold of her hands, she added. 'You can stay as long as you want.'

The warm, soft, white skin touching hers was all it took for Louise to burst into tears.

Alice sat quietly beside her daughter, giving her time to calm down and drink her tea before speaking. 'C'mon. Let's take your bag upstairs.' She tugged at Louise's hand, pulling her up from the seat. George reached for the poker and began stirring the coal in the grate creating an explosion of sparks as the coal hissed and spat.

Louise opened her mouth to speak to him, but his back was turned resolutely against her. She followed her mother into the hall and stepped onto the faded, patterned runner on the stairs. The same runner her feet had raced over every day of her life until she'd left home ten years ago.

'I s'pose I'd better bank it up. She'll be wanting a bath next,' he shouted after them.

The words sounded gruff, but a shadow of a smile crept across Louise's face as she remembered him using those same words every Friday night when she would shovel her tea down and race upstairs to get ready for a night out with her friend, Barbara. She pictured herself, running back down to him, kissing his cheek and whispering in his ear. "Thanks, Dad. You're the best." He'd turn and waft her away with his hands. "Get on with you", he'd mumble, then she'd dash back upstairs as happy as it was possible to be.

Alice held the bedroom door open as Louise lugged her suitcase inside and dropped it down onto the purple, shag-pile carpet. Looking around, she felt as if she had never left. The room was exactly as it was the last time she had seen it. 'Oh, Mum.'

'I wanted it to stay as it was until you got home,' her mum said.

Louise looked at the David Cassidy posters on the wall, the little trolls with bright coloured hair in a range of colours; standing to attention along the windowsill. Sitting on the edge of the bed, gripping the mattress, she was hardly able to see anything through the puddles swimming around her eyes. 'I thought you would have thrown it all away. Redecorated. I didn't expect...deserve...'

'You're my daughter,' said Alice. 'This is your home.' Turning to leave, she added. 'You take as long as you want. Come down when you're ready.'

Louise lay down on the bed and stared up at the ceiling. She looked at her watch. Visiting was at seven.

*

She opened her eyes; it was pitch black. She flinched and sat up. What time was it? He'd be back soon. Louise reached out for her watch. It wasn't there. She snatched at her wrist and, feeling the metal strap, relaxed and let her breath out slowly. She hadn't taken it off. While she fumbled for the bedside light, the bedroom door opened and light flooded in from the landing.

'I'm coming,' she said, practically diving from the bed, feeling dizzy as the blood rushed from her head.

'It's alright. No rush. I've brought you a cup of tea.'

'Mum?' Louise remembered where she was. She took the cup and saucer and put them down on the pine, bedside cabinet. 'What time is it?'

'Six o'clock. I've run a bath for you. We'll eat at seven. Cold beef and salad okay?'

Louise checked her watch. 'I think that will be alright. Thank you,' she said, reaching out her hand. Her mum squeezed it gently and went back downstairs.

Louise got out of bed and opened her suitcase, taking out her cosmetics bag. She unzipped it and took out some cleanser and cotton wool balls. Sitting down at her dressing table, she took a hairbrush from her old vanity case, unclipped her long blonde hair and brushed it. Her perfect makeup was smudged around her eyes and made her face look clownish, ugly. Looking in the mirror, she cleaned up her face and saw only a faint shadow of the girl who ran off with the handsome fashion scout so long ago. She could see him now, still feel his hand tight around her wrist as he lay on the trolley, ready to go down to the theatre. *"You'll be back here in time for visiting."*

Louise stripped and reached for her old, pink fluffy dressing gown from behind the door and put it on. It made her feel like a teenager again, flooding her mind with memories. It was soft and gentle on her skin, but it was enormous, falling off her narrow shoulders like a man's coat that had been put on a child's hanger by mistake. Lifting the collar up around her face, she breathed in deeply. Pure Flakes. Mum always washed with Pure Soap Flakes. It was her favourite brand. Even in the twin tub. Always said powder didn't dissolve properly on delicate fabrics. She looked on the bookshelves above the dresser to see if there was anything worth reading in the bath. There were the books for her A-level studies, some childhood favourites and some classics her father had bought her when she'd said she was taking English Lit. He had been so proud of her. "My little girl is going to university" he'd brag to anyone who'd listen. "She'll be the first in our family." She stroked the spines of the unopened books, feeling the hurt he must have gone through when she had let him down so badly. There were a couple of copies of Jackie on the edge of the bottom shelf. Reaching for one, she noticed a scrapbook beneath the magazines.

She pulled it down and opened it to see a photo of herself staring out from a newspaper article, David watching her from the front row. The headline read: *Fashion Scout, David Loach hits the jackpot as his new model, Louise Kennedy causes a stir on the London catwalk.* The photo had been taken at her first time at the London Fashion Week show. Mum must have cut it out and saved it. Turning the pages, clipping after clipping from Vogue, Elle and every national newspaper filled the leaves. She remembered a journalist coming to interview them in their luxury apartment. The photo showed them sitting on the white leather sofa that was always so cold, David's arm tight around her waist. Snapping the scrapbook closed, Louise pinned up her hair again and left the bedroom.

As she crept across the landing, she heard her mum and dad talking downstairs

'You're a fool, Alice. Not a word for nigh-on ten years and she waltzes in here, turns on the waterworks and expects everything to be just the same.'

'I'm so worried, George. Something's not right. She's like a skeleton.'

'Have you heard yourself? She's turned her back on him exactly like she did with us. Why did she always send him to answer the phone? Eh? Couldn't have been clearer the last time she actually deigned to speak to us. *"I'm so sorry. Time seems to go so quickly. I'll try harder."* You'll see.'

The anger and hurt in his voice as he mocked hers was unbearable. Louise had never wanted to hurt them; she had missed them both so much. She retreated to the steam-filled bathroom where their voices became an indecipherable murmur. Taking the watch off her wrist, she checked the time. Twenty past six. How long was she allowed?

Sinking through the soft bubbles and into the warm water, she closed her eyes and bit down on her lip until the initial sting subsided, finally wallowing in the sheer bliss of soaking in a hot bath. It had been such a long time. Closing her eyes, she started to drift off.

There was a light tap on the door.

Louise was startled from her thoughts. It had never occurred to her to lock it. Not after so long.

'Can I come in?' Alice peered around the door. 'I've warmed a towel by the fire,' she said, smiling and placing it on the closed toilet lid. Her smiled dwindled, and when she spoke again, it came out as a whisper. She tried to control the sudden tremble in her voice. 'I bet you came home so I could feed you up.'

Louise sat up, covering her breasts with her hands, almost crying out as the kindness in her mother's voice wrapped itself around her.

'Would you like me to wash your back?'

Louise shook her head, lying down again, covering herself with bubbles.

Alice sat on the edge of the bath. 'I could wash your hair if you like?'

Louise wanted to cry, wanted her mum to hold her, rock her, make everything the way it used to be. She looked at the watch lying on the shelf below the bathroom cabinet.

'You're right,' said her mum, standing up. 'Time is getting on. I'll see you downstairs shortly.'

Alice stroked her daughter's arm as she turned away.

Louise waited until she heard her mother's footsteps on the stairs before standing up. She reached for the towel, wrapped it around her body and made her way back into the bedroom. Remembering her watch, she dashed back to the bathroom and retrieved it. How long had she been out of the bath? Ten minutes she'd asked for. Was there time to dress and do her hair? She let the towel drop around her ankles and fastened the watch on to her wrist. Bending over the suitcase, she pulled out some underwear: a pale-green, cashmere sweater and a pair of Calvin Klein jeans and laid them on the bed. Would these be alright? She'd better hurry. Slipping her arms through the narrow straps of her bra, she heard a loud gasp and spun around to see her mother standing in the doorway with her hand over her mouth, her eyes brimming and shiny with tears.

'Oh my goodness! What has he done to you?'

Louise tried to cover her buttocks with her hands. The telephone in the hallway began to ring. Louise looked at her watch. Five past seven. She shrank back and dropped to the floor, curling into a ball.

12 SWEET AND SOUR

2016

It was hot and dry, the streets dusty. The air thick with the sound of cars and the choking smell of diesel fumes. Crossing the high street, Petra slipped down a side road, leaving the noise of the traffic behind her. She sighed, wiping her forehead with the back of her hand. Delving into her bag, she lifted out the punnet and popped a fresh strawberry into her mouth. Not quite the same taste as the cherries she used to pick back home, but welcome to her parched tongue.

'Hey! Pole! Yeah, you. When you goin' home?'

No. Please. Not today.

'This is my home,' she answered. 'I've lived here for five years.'

The small group of boys stood on the corner of her street, drinking from cans and smoking roll-ups. They couldn't have been any more than seventeen or eighteen.

'Ain't you heard? We're leaving the EU, innit, so you'd better pack your bags.'

Petra tried to walk around them, desperate to get home and take a shower. Then she could put her feet up and enjoy a long, cold drink.

They blocked her way. She stepped off the kerb, over the litter-strewn gutter and attempted to walk along the road, but they mimicked every move she made.

The one in the camouflage jacket and army boots, who had shouted first, came closer. His face was screwed up and sneering as he looked down at her. His trousers were so low; Petra could virtually see all of his dirty underwear. He knocked the punnet from her hands.

'Weren't you listenin'?'

Petra lifted her chin and looked straight up into his eyes. 'What do you want?'

'I want,' he said, poking her shoulder with his forefinger. 'I want to know when you're going to pack your bags and fuck off home. Then me and my squad might have a job to go to.'

'You don't want my job,' she said. 'It is hard work.' She pushed his hand away and attempted to pass again.

'Bollocks,' said an even taller boy, taking over from his friend. He had a lank, brown fringe covering half his face in an effort to hide cheeks that blazed with overripe berries of acne. 'You lot make me crazy, innit.'

Petra felt the anger burn in her chest. For a moment, it overtook the fear. 'Alright,' she said. 'There are jobs where I work. Many more since the Referendum. Since you make my friends leave.' Grabbing the boy's arm, she headed back in the direction she had come from. 'Come. Walk with me. There are jobs for all of you.' She hoped her boss, Steve, would offer them something. He didn't like shirkers.

Fringe Boy snatched himself free, but let her walk ahead. They all taunted her as she strode on, mimicking the way her arms were swinging purposefully at her sides, dancing in front of her, prodding, poking.

Dirty Underwear said. 'You'd better not be lying bitch.'

Petra carried on regardless. She tried to imagine she was coming home from the cherry harvest in Szomolya. She would have eaten too many of the sour fruits and would be groaning with tummy-ache. Her tummy hurt now.

A girl with long, dyed-black hair crossed the street and joined them. She was wearing a midriff shirt and denim shorts that left her swollen belly bulging and her bottom cheeks on display.

'Hey, Bae. What's happenin?' she asked, linking Fringe Boy's arm. 'You better not be hooking up with this slag.'

'What? When I got you, Chels?' he said wrapping his arm around her neck and kissing her.

Petra had seen Chelsea before. She lived on the same street. Petra had always felt sadness for the girl's mother when she'd seen them arguing on the doorstep. She couldn't understand why the daughter was so disrespectful.

'What sort of a style d'ya call this? Horsetail?' Petra tried not to react as the girl poked her back and tugged on her blonde plait. 'Hey! Don't you ignore me, Slag!'

She hoped there would still be people at work, finishing the packing. Maybe Andras wouldn't have left with the delivery yet. He had said he would probably be late home to the little-terraced house they rented.

As they came back into the main road, an elderly woman shuffled past, tripping in her haste. The boys laughed. A group of schoolchildren stood outside the local takeaway. They nudged each other and whispered, trying not to draw the attention of the gang on themselves. Petra held her head high as they walked the streets, back to the edge of town.

*

The flat fields spread out before them. Mile after mile after mile of strawberries. If only she were back home. Out on her father's farm, the warm summer breeze caressing her skin as she tended to the pigs and geese.

She wanted to run but knew they would catch her. She must stay calm. This was nothing like the happy tiredness after the cherry harvest where everyone walked home together, laughing and joking. More and more, she has to tell herself she has made the right decision, how the opportunities would make it all worth the hard work.

She passed through an open gate and made her way between the rows of fruit. Nearly there.

Turning to face the boys who had stopped at the edge of the field, she smiled, hands on her hips, lifting her voice. 'Here. Here is work. Come. I will take you to my boss.'

Dirty Underpants snorted. 'Christ. I thought you meant a proper job. If you think we're going to break our backs picking strawberries—'

'You don't want work?' Petra shrugged and shook her head. 'You Scottish boys. You are so lazy.'

Dirt Underpants' eyes narrowed. 'We ain't bleedin' Scottish, you daft cow.'

'No? I am not Polish, but you call me Pole.' She was

feeling braver, tilting her chin as she continued. 'I am from Hungary.' She spread her arms out wide. 'You are little boys, you don't know anything.'

Dirty Underpants spat then wiped his mouth with his sleeve. 'You think yoo's lit don't you?' He entered the field and walked towards her, grinning. The rest of the gang followed him. 'Bet you don't know what happens next.'

Petra stepped backwards, stumbling on the uneven ground. 'My friends are not far. They will come.'

Dirty Underpants lurched forward, grabbed her arm and pulled a knife from his pocket. 'Know what this is for? Cutting up Hungary girls and feeding them to this hungry squad.' The others laughed. He pushed his forehead hard up against hers. 'We's all a bit thirsty too, like. Know what I mean? Aint been no Smash today.' He held the blade of his knife to her chin. It was sharp against her skin. His breath smelled sour from cigarettes and beer. 'You lads are thirsty, innit? On your back, bitch.'

Petra's heart thudded in her chest. Her head was spinning. The boys were all around her now, chanting. 'Smash. Smash. Smash.'

Petra's hands shielded her stomach. She searched Chelsea's eyes for any sense of understanding, desperate for a sign, any sign of compassion in the girl.

Chelsea pulled at Fringe Boy. 'Don't! We need the money. Mam says we can live with her after the kid's born. We'll need stuff. A pram thing innit?'

Fringe Boy turned to the girl. Unsure.

'Yoos do what yer like. I'm havin' some,' said Dirty Underpants.

Fringe Boy blocked his way. 'Chels is right. We all need it. My mam is havin' to use the food bank.'

Petra took a deep breath. 'Please come,' she said to the boys. 'I promise there will be work.'

The boys looked up the field, hesitating. There were a few grumbles before they moved aside and let her pass. They followed close behind as Petra turned her back on them and walked on. Fringe Boy and Chelsea joined them.

Dirty Underpants stayed where he was. 'Do what you like, losers. I'm not doing dirty immigrant work,' he said and walked back towards the gate.

Petra could see some of her work colleagues up ahead. Steve's wife, Barbara stopped working and shielded her eyes against the sun before waving at Petra.

She waved back, half walking, half running until she was standing by Barbara's side. Petra admired the woman who still worked as hard as everyone even though she was now in her sixties.

The gang hung back a little. Petra's voice trembled slightly as she asked if there was work for them, adding that the boy with the girlfriend was definitely in most need.

Barbara looked at Petra and frowned. Petra forced a smile and mouthed that she was alright. Barbara squeezed her hand and turned to the group. 'How many of you are prepared to put the hours in? It's back-breaking work and long days until the harvest is in.'

Chelsea was the first to answer. 'We'll work hard,' she said, pulling Fringe boy by the hand and leading him forward. 'We need the money, innit?'

'Like she said,' another boy added. They all followed Chelsea.

'Right, then. You'd better follow me to the office. I'll give you some forms to fill in at home. Anyone who turns up at seven on the dot in the morning has got a job.' Barbara led them away.

Petra's closest friends had gone back to Hungary. She missed them. Perhaps it would have been better to have gone home for a visit during her holidays from the food processing factory instead of taking on the strawberry picking. It would have been good to have seen see her parents. Gone to the cherry festival in Szomolya. She thought of the big celebration when all the harvesting was done, everyone in the village contributing what they could afford in food and drink. She could practically taste the tart, luscious fruit. Her mother made the best sour-cherry soup in the world.

She hoped Andras would still be working in the despatch shed. She hoped he would understand. Her hand stroked the gentle swelling of her stomach.

13 LIFE STYLIST

1990

'So what did Norman say?' asked Sonia as she pinned the last roller in the wiry grey hair. She was chatting to Dot's reflection through the mirror. Two sparkling eyes looked back at her out of a lifetime's laughter wrinkles.

'Not on your Nelly, that's what he said.'

'I'm not surprised. Can you imagine? Your Norman bungee jumping?' Sonia laughed out loud at the thought. 'It'll take around 15 minutes, Dot. Can I get you a cuppa?' Dot smiled in response.

Sonia finished blow-drying another customer's hair and a little while later, ushered Dot over to the washbasin. She rinsed her hair thoroughly and applied the neutraliser. Once Dot was ensconced with a coffee and a magazine, Sonia nipped into the back room for a breather. It was three o' clock and she hadn't even had a lunch break yet. It was always like this the week before Christmas. Dot was a regular, every week come rain or shine, a wash and blow dry, a perm every three months and a tale about Norman's latest calamity. Norman seemed to be Dot's life. She obviously adored the man unconditionally. "Unconditionally". That's what John had said. She remembered the row they had this morning.

*

'Why can't you do the shopping? You know I'll have to work extra hours for the next week.' Sonia left John sitting at the kitchen table and went to the bottom of the stairs. 'C'mon you two. Breakfast's ready' she called up to her children.

'Because I've got a meeting with David Sones about the expansion plans. Besides,' he said, 'it's your job.'

Sonia didn't rise to the comment. Tom and Katy ran down the stairs and into the kitchen.

'I can make you a list. You can do it on your way home from work tomorrow. You finish early enough.' Sonia could feel her face beginning to flush as she poured his coffee, almost spilling it as she slammed it down in front of him. The children looked at her. 'Eat your cereal Katy; you haven't got time to read your kindle. Have you got football practice tonight Tom? Let me know whether to make tea for you or not. Text me before I leave work.' she turned back to John.' Well?'

'Why can't you do it on Sunday morning when I'm

playing golf?' John picked up his briefcase and headed for the door.

'Because I may have to work Sunday as well,' she hissed, following him into the hall. 'For goodness sake. Can't you do one small thing for me for a change? Work and Golf, that's all you think about.'

'I am who I am Sonia,' He leaned over her, puckering his lips,' You know that. Stop scowling and give me a kiss!' She pushed him away.

'You're impossible. I'm sick of you putting me last. Don't you think I have enough to do? Why can't you give me a hand once in a while?' Sonia stomped back to the kitchen.

'I thought you loved me unconditionally? That's what you used to say. Love you. Bye.' The door slammed.

'Bye Dad.' shouted the kids in unison.

Sonia stood at the kitchen sink with her back to the children as she wiped away the angry tears. 'He's so selfish,' she muttered under her breath.

*

Sonia finished her coffee and usual cheese sandwich before going back into the salon and

'Right Dot, let's check your hair.' She undid one roller and examined the curl. 'Yes, it's fine.'

Sonia eased Dot's head back so that her head was over the basin. She tucked a rolled towel behind her neck for comfort before rinsing and washing the neutraliser out.

'I love this bit,' said Dot. 'It's heaven to get all the rollers out.'

Sonia laughed. 'You always say that. Everyone hates the rollers.' She wrapped a towel around Dot's hair and helped her sit up again. 'Right! Let's get you back over there for the final round.'

Dot limped across the room and settled herself back in the seat in front of the mirror. She looked through the glass at Sonia who was plugging the hair dryer into the socket on the wall next to her.

'Something the matter pet?' she asked, frowning.

Sonia forced a smile as she looked into the mirror. 'Oh, nothing. Had a few words with John this morning.'

'Nothing serious, I hope?'

'No. I needed a bit of help from him. But it seems he's too busy as usual.'

'Busy at the golf club? My Norman was never as

busy as when he wanted to go to the darts. I used to go on at him all the time. "Married to that darts team you." Never did any good though. Still, it kept him happy and out of my hair most of the time. He was lost when he first retired. The army was his life. '

Sonia picked up her scissors and set about styling and cutting the mop of curls on Dot's head. 'I don't want John out of my hair. I just need his help.' she said. 'It's the Christmas rush. Never seem to get a minute to do things at home or do any shopping. He could help a bit.'

Dot smiled, sympathetically. 'You should try and make a bit of time for yourself. Do something you want to do. I remember taking up singing. I joined St Martin's choir.'

'Chance would be a fine thing,' she said, putting her hands on Dot's shoulders. 'There's so much to do.'

'Life's for living Sonia. The jobs get done eventually. John works longs hours doesn't he?'

'Yes, of course, he does, but so do I.' Sonia sighed. 'I used to love art at school.' She stretched the curls either side of Dot's face checking the length was equal.

'There you go then.' Dot grinned at Sonia's reflection.

'Chance would be a fine thing.'

'For goodness sake! Make it happen, Sonia.'

Sonia sighed. 'I'd love to take it up again. Nothing major, maybe watercolours.'

'It'll do you good. If you can't beat 'em, join 'em I always say. Did our marriage a world of good. He stopped taking me for granted, even came to some of the concerts I did.'

Sonia's mind was in a whirl as she plugged in the hairdryer. She would take up a hobby. He'd have to get used to waiting for things, so would the kids. She had a life too.

*

John closed the front door and came through to the kitchen. Sonia was laying the table for tea. The cutlery clattered on the wood surface as she threw it down.

'Hi, sweetheart.' He kissed the back of her neck and put his arms around her waist, squeezing lightly. 'Had a good day?'

She pushed his hands away and span around to face him. Her face was flushed, her voice sharp. 'A nice day? I've been rushed off my feet as usual. About the shopping—'

'About that...I've had an idea,' he interrupted, pulling her to him again. 'We can do it online and get it delivered to the door.'

'Oh Yes. And you'll be happy paying all those delivery charges.' she spat, jerking her head back and glaring up at him. 'Money no object all of a sudden?'

He held on to her, his voice low and soothing. 'We'll make savings on petrol, and you won't get stuck in traffic or have to lug all those bags about anymore. I know I can be a bit selfish sometimes.'

'That would save time, I suppose.'

He felt her body relax a little.

'I've been thinking about joining an art class,' she said tentatively. 'What do you think?'

'I think that's a brilliant idea. It's about time you had a hobby.' John kissed the top of her head, breathing in the delicate perfume of her hair. He stayed silent for a moment or two. 'So it's okay if I go to the golf club on Sunday?'

She couldn't stop the grin from forming on her lips as she batted his arm. 'Yes. But don't expect lunch to be ready when you get back. I'm working. Don't forget.'

'No problem,' he said, stepping back and beaming at her. 'Why don't you and the kids meet me at the club when you've finished. We can eat there.'

'That sounds good. By the way. I love you.'

'Unconditionally?'

'Unconditionally.'

14 HOLDING ON TO FAITH

1865

'Good morning, Father.' I am a little wary as I place his breakfast before him. The skin beneath his eyes is puffed and bruised as a plum. His moustache and hair are tousled. He is usually meticulous about his grooming. His eyes are too bright, piercing, twitching, his skin dark and clammy. 'Shall I say grace this morning?'

'What?' He shakes his head as if trying to recover himself from a dream. 'No. No, Faith. I will do it.' He closes his eyes, raising his long, veined hands to the heavens. 'Dear Lord, I thank you for your inspiration. For showing me the way last evening. You have given me much to think about on this day. Amen.' He opens his eyes and looks at me, his smile broad, unfamiliar. 'Faith, there is much work to do today and I will need your help.' He hurries his junket, spilling a little on his napkin.

Help? He eyes me carefully. I know he looks for

any sign of fear. I keep my face dull and look directly into those dark pools that seem to swallow me whole. He smiles again.

'I need you to go into town. You may leave the house at ten of the hour and be over the threshold again by twelve. I will list the items you must fetch. You will bring no more, no less.'

Going directly to the mahogany desk where he writes his letters and keeps the household bills, which now stand high and tottering as an old bent lady, he takes up a quill and scribbles swiftly. My heart thuds at the thought of freedom for two, whole hours.

He leaves the list on his desk, along with two, shiny shilling pieces and strides across the room to the large oak door of his laboratory. Without turning his head, he says. 'Remember, Faith. Not one thing more. Not one thing less.' He puts the key in the lock and disappears.

I rush to the desk and take up the list. I eventually untangle his cypher and read it out loud: One bottle of Godfrey's cordial, One bottle of Opium Vapour oil, One troy ounce of Laudanum Tincture and...

What? That cannot be what he means, can it?

'One young homeless man from the poorer part of the town... Offer him supper at our table.'

Has my father gone mad? How can he ask

something like this of me?

*

I step out of the front door of Bridge House and onto the drive. The sun is shining and I stop on the bridge to look down at the river. Light splashes through the crystal clear water as it races over the worn pebbles. Minnows dart in the shallows and a brown trout wriggles its tail, its face rummages into the fine gravel, looking for larvae. My mood is high at the outset, but walking along the busy high street of Blackdale brings memories of my mother flooding back. Hand in hand we had strolled along, stopping at the haberdashery for ribbons, ordering a brace of pheasant and two large rabbits from Mr Caldwell, the butcher and one day we had gone to see if the bolt of silk cloth had been delivered to Miss Applethwaite, the seamstress. I see her ever smiling face, her striking, green eyes, the only things I inherited from her. More and more of late, I have remembered her whispered bedtime stories. She would tell me of the balls she attended as a debutante, the stunning dresses, the music and dancing, carriage rides through the park. How Father, such an eminent physician, had swept her off her feet. I remember how her face used to light up with happiness when she told me. Where did those dresses go? Where did that loving father go? Did his love and kindness die with my mother as she gave birth three years ago? I miss the sibling I was never allowed to see.

Tears begin to sting, and I dash them away as I see the apple-cheeked, Mrs Proctor walking towards me. I tug on my muslin bonnet, so it shades my eyes and gather my cloak about me.

'Good morning, Miss Ryder. Goodness, how you have grown, quite the young lady and so like your dear departed mother, Constance. Such a wonderfully gracious lady. How is your dear father? We have not seen him in the town of late.' Her beady eyes search mine.

'He...he is very well, thank you.' I look away, my lips trembling.

'Well. Must get on. Things to attend to.' She scuttles away, unsettled by my show of emotion in public.

I move along quickly, not looking where I am going, tears running into my mouth, salty. A carriage and four clatters along the street towards me. My head is spinning.

Something crashes into me. I cry out as I'm thrown full circle, landing in a heap on the pavement.

'So sorry, Miss. I thought you were about to... here, let me help you.'

Two strong hands lift me to my feet. I immediately brush my skirts down, too embarrassed to see who my rescuer is. 'Thank you, Sir. I am fine.'

'It is a long time since anyone referred to me as a gentleman.' He laughs loudly. His voice is warm. I look up and see a pair of brown eyes, sparkling with mischief. His broad face and smile are practically hidden beneath an unkempt beard and moustache. His coat is soiled and ragged, but the cut is fine. His voice suggests an education.

I do not feel afraid. Returning my basket to me, he doffs an imaginary hat. His gesture makes me smile.'See! That is much better.' My cheeks burn. 'So glad to have met you,' he adds and starts to walk away.

'Wait! Please wait,' I call after him.

*

The change in Father is astonishing. His usual taciturn manner has disappeared. The gentleman, Mr Webb, Richard has been here for only a few hours, filling the house with conversation.

Mr Webb talks of his path to ruin, how his drinking turned him into a beast. Father grins at the choice of words.

'I would not see a fellow student of Oxford out on the streets. Your path to drink has brought you to us, allowing your path to righteousness to begin. I think we shall be well suited. You will work alongside me, Richard in return for board and lodging.' Father holds his hand up to silence whatever response Mr Webb had in mind. 'Please remember my research is entirely confidential and of course,' He nods to stress his point. 'You must not, under any circumstances, discuss anything that happens beyond the laboratory door. I must also insist you embrace our beliefs while you are under my roof. Faith is well versed in the scriptures and she will teach you in the evenings after supper.'

My cheeks are on fire as our guest looks to me for confirmation.

'I would be more than willing, Mr Webb if it is what you wish.'

Father slams his fist on to the table. 'We are talking about conditions, Faith. Not wishes.'

'Of course, Father,' I answer, lowering my gaze.

Richards smiles in my direction. The candles on the dining table add a warm glow to his face and reflect in his beautiful eyes.

'Your conditions suit me well, Sir. I look forward to your daughter putting me on the right path.' I hear the warmth in his words... and almost...what is that? Laughter? We eat the rest of our meal in silence, but my heart beats in my ears. I fear it is as loud as the tick of the grandfather clock standing in the hall.

After supper, my father retires to his chair by the fire and takes out his Sacred Writ. I sit at his feet, Richard takes the other armchair, listening alongside me as father reads the stories aloud. Richard says he has not heard of such scriptures before and Father tells him we belong to a small religious group.

'We do not follow our dear Queen's faith, even though she is most pious in her Lutheran ways. The Brotherhood has written down the real meaning of the Bible, and this Sacred Writ is the path we must follow, Richard.'

I watch the coals glow and spark; the fountains of red flame, shower the blackened sides of the chimney. I cling to the warmth. Father talks to Richard about his work. I try not to listen as he explains how he studies and examines his 'beautiful arachnids' under a microscope. Sometimes I dream the vile creatures have escaped and herd me into a corner, racing up my legs to bite me, eat me. It makes my skin feel so alive that I cannot help shaking.

Father notices. 'Fear is a weakness, Faith. Your mother was weak.' I wish he would not say such things. Not in front of a stranger. *How can dying in childbirth be a weakness?* 'It is time you retired,' he adds.

I get up from the faded, woven rug, thinking of all tomorrow's chores. Lighting a taper in the fire, I transfer the flame to a candle. As I make my way up the stairs, my shadow, flickers, dances and stretches across the walls and ceiling. *How thin it looks*. I pull the candle low and search the dark corners of each step for any escapees. Once in my room, I check every nook and cranny: under the bed, even in the chamber pot. Only when I have done this can I lie down and think about the young man who has made the house come alive again.

*

It is the third morning since he came. I have finished preparing breakfast as Father comes down the stairs, followed by Mr Webb who looks most handsome now I have laundered his coat.

'Good morning, Father. Good morning, Mr Webb. I hope you have slept well.' The smile on my face must give my emotions away.

Father insists I say grace today. Swallowing hard to steady my nerves, I recite the prayer aloud.

'Dear Lord, we thank Thee for all Thou doth lay before us. For your help in guiding my father in his work. For keeping me in your thoughts and ensuring I am an obedient daughter who will always serve my father well. I...the words have slipped away. *Please, please let me remember,* I am... I am the servant of your holy will. I will remain pure in all ways until my father directs me in the path of holy matrimony to a man he deems appropriate.'

Richard is staring at me when I open my eyes. When he has finished eating, he says it is the best breakfast he has ever tasted. I know he only flatters, but I bathe in his voice and drown in his smiling eyes.

My spirits are lifted as they disappear through the heavy oak door and into the laboratory, knowing I will see him again this evening. I start about my chores and find I am humming little ditties my mother taught me as I helped her with the housework such a long time ago. Life is suddenly much sweeter.

*

Tonight we have had the pleasure of Richard's company for more than two weeks. When we have finished the teaching, which I have been more than glad to administer nightly since he first arrived, he passes a note to me along with the holy book. I take it nervously as his hand touches mine so softly it sends a shiver up my arm. Slipping it into my pocket, I carry the dirty dishes through to the scullery and put some water on top of the range to boil. My hands are shaking as I read.

Dearest, Faith

Please tell me why your father treats you so cruelly? How can I help to change this?

Richard.

Happiness erupts from within, overflowing, making

my heart flutter so. I am sure I will faint at any minute. I resolve to write and tell him everything: how when he lost my mother, my father had said she was too weak to carry all the children he desired; how he insisted he must give up his practice and concentrate fully on his experiments. That all these things had meant less income so my father had dismissed the servants saying we must both toil and make sacrifices, channelling all feelings of love towards our Lord.

*

The weeks are flying by. I cannot fight my feelings for Richard. This evening, when he finally emerges from the laboratory, I am so hungry. Not for food but for his company.

My father seems quite genial as we sit down for supper. Richard breathes in the aroma as I remove the lid from the tureen and ladle the mutton broth into the bowls. He seems to be savouring every mouthful. It pleases me much that he enjoys my cooking.

Father eats sporadically, too involved in what he has to say to Richard to notice what he is eating.

'They are creatures of such prowess. It is only their size that limits their potential,' says Father.

'Indeed, Sir. They could be most powerful,' Richard says.

'What a different world that would be,' Father quips, grinning wildly.

I have begun to notice of late that Richard's face radiates a dark shine as if he has spent too long in the sun. It is the same pallor as my father displays. It must be a side effect of working under the laboratory lights.

The conversation flows, and after lessons, Father suggests Richard help me with the dishes. I can hardly control my excitement as we carry everything into the scullery.

Standing close together at the sink, I feel the heat from his body, smell the musky scent of his skin. He slides his hand around my waist, spins me around and pulls me close.

'I think I am in love with you, Faith,' he whispers. 'I want to wrap you up and hold you tight, so you might never escape.'

I look up into his eyes. His black pupils are so dilated, I cannot see the rich brown of his irises. His dark lips meet mine. The bristles on his beard prickle my cheeks and chin. His hand slides up to the back of my neck, and I should try to pull away, but he pushes his tongue into my mouth. He tastes of the rich broth and the sweet cherries in the pie I made and...something bitter? Medicinal? It reminds me of Father. I succumb to his kisses as a deep shudder ripples through my body.

We part, both gasping for breath and I flush with shame. Embarrassed. I turn my attention back to the dishes.

*

Their faces are solemn as they come out of the laboratory tonight. *What are they thinking? Has Father refused?* Panic swallows my words. I cannot greet them.

'You may say grace,' Father says and takes his seat.

I tremble as I eventually find my voice, stuttering at each syllable.

Sitting at the table, I find the silence unbearable. *Say it and destroy my life forever. Have I not done penance enough?*

'Faith, I have something to tell you.' Father looks at me, without smiling. 'Richard has asked for your hand in marriage.' He pauses. I close my eyes and expect the worst. 'I have agreed to his proposal but—' He raises his hand to silence me, but I rush from my seat and throw my arms around his neck.

'Thank you. Oh, thank you, dearest Father.'

'Enough,' he says, removing my arms and pushing me away. 'There are conditions...you will both remain in this house after the wedding and Richard must continue his duties as my apprentice. Is that clear?' He looks at

Richard for assent.

'Of course. I would not wish it any other way, Sir.'

'I will arrange for someone from the Brotherhood to come tomorrow to conduct the wedding ceremony. You will avow your pledge of obedience beforehand, Richard. There will be no requirement for guests or fanciful clothes.' His look shows the conversation is at an end. 'It is time for Richard's lesson, Faith.'

Turning to Richard for comfort, I see he has already picked up the Sacred Writ and is reading it as if nothing has happened. *No dress? No maid of honour? No new home?*

After lessons, Richard takes my arm and leads me through to the scullery. I am so confused. Should I be happy or sad?

'Don't be upset, my dearest. We have each other and that is what is important,' he says, rolling up his sleeves.

The vast number of fine dark hairs which appear to have grown on his forearms are now as dark as his face. A violent, cold shiver shudders down my spine. His eyebrows have disappeared; his forehead is bulging. Several orbs are pushing against the translucent skin, twitching. Like the eyes in a nest of newborn mice, I once discovered in the attic.

'But why must we stay here?' I stutter, backing across the room.

'It was part of the agreement. Your father says I play a vital role in his experiments. He is desperate for us to be married and provide him with lots of little ones to run around the house. Little ones your mother failed to provide. Come!' He grips my hand and leads me to two small stools in the corner of the kitchen. 'No more fear. Fear is a weakness, Faith.' He leans forward to kiss me. That same medicinal smell. Beneath the natural bristles of his beard, two sharp protuberances push against my chin. I shake as a childhood rhyme Father used to recite, plays inside my head...

Little Miss Ryder

a fine-looking girl,

who had no mother to guide her.

Sat down on a stool,

the poor little fool,

and was kissed by a large, handsome spider.

****

ACKNOWLEDGMENTS

I would like to say thank you so much to the following people:

To all the long term members of The Next Chapter Writing Group: Dolores Newton, Sandy Kell, Ken Mathers, Pamela Holliday, Svein Hagen and Hazel Goss for all the support and feedback they have given me over the years. Hazel and I have also supported one another when we have run author events. We make a great team.

Imogen Clark, a dear friend I met while studying with the Open University for believing in me and always there with the right words to get me going again when I faltered and lost confidence.

Gerry Ryan for all her support and guidance as a tutor while studying with the OCA.

Jackie Buxton for her excellent editing skills.

ABOUT THE AUTHOR

C J Richardson lives in a small village in North Yorkshire with her husband. This is the second time around for both of them and they have six grown up children a growing number of grandchildren.

She started writing seriously when she retired from a career in accountancy in 2008. Firstly joining a beginners class and then, along with some fellow students, forming a writing group THE NEXT CHAPTER . We meet regularly to share our work and also to critique and help each other.

She has studied with the OU and gained a distinction for her year three course in Creative Writing. She is currently studying with OCA for a BA in creative writing.

Website: http: //www.cjrichardsonwriter.com/

Facebook : https://www.facebook.com/cjrichardsonwriter/

Twitter: https://twitter.com/cjrichardsonwr

Other Titles by this Author

Can Martha stay faithful to her husband fighting in the trenches when his brother is the one who stole her heart and much more?

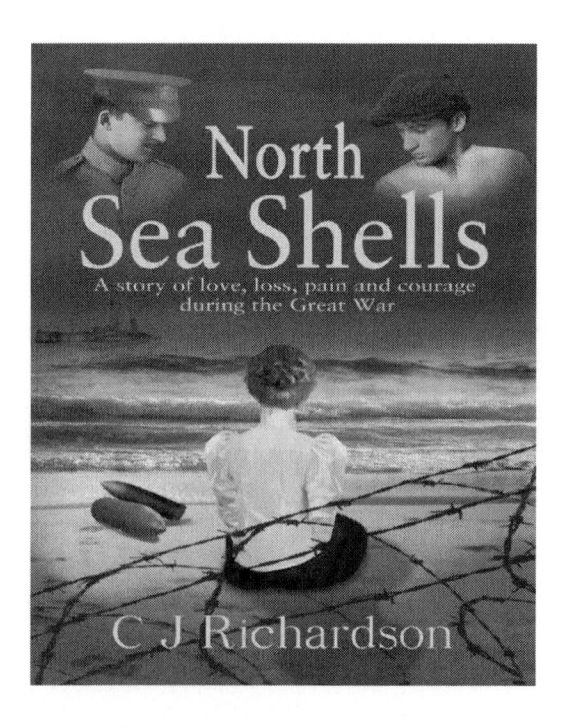

NORTH SEA SHELLS

Available at https://www.amazon.co.uk/North-Sea-Shells-C-Richardson/

Printed in Poland
by Amazon Fulfillment
Poland Sp. z o.o., Wrocław